THE LADY GRACE
MYSTERIES

D0281094

Also available in
THE LADY GRACE MYSTERIES series

ASSASSIN
BETRAYAL
CONSPIRACY
DECEPTION
EXILE
FEUD
GOLD!
HAUNTED
INTRIGUE
JINX

❀

Coming soon
LOOT

THE LADY GRACE
MYSTERIES

KEYS

Grace Cavendish

Jan Burchett and Sara Vogler are writing as Grace Cavendish

RED FOX

THE LADY GRACE MYSTERIES: KEYS
A RED FOX BOOK 978 1 862 30421 5

Published in Great Britain by Red Fox,
an imprint of Random House Children's Books
A Random House Group Company

This edition published 2009

1 3 5 7 9 10 8 6 4 2

Series created by Working Partners Ltd
Copyright © Working Partners Ltd, 2009
Cover illustration by Paul Finn

The Random House Group Limited makes every effort to ensure that the papers
used in its books are made from trees that have been legally sourced from well-managed
and credibly certified forests. Our paper procurement policy can be found at:
www.randomhouse.co.uk/paper.htm

Set in Bembo

Red Fox Books are published by Random House Children's Books,
61–63 Uxbridge Road, London W5 5SA

www.kidsatrandomhouse.co.uk
www.rbooks.co.uk

Addresses for companies within The Random House Group Limited can be found at:
www.randomhouse.co.uk/offices.htm

A CIP catalogue record for this book is available from the British Library.

Printed in the UK by CPI Bookmarque, Croydon, CR0 4TD

For Sophie Groome,
a devoted Lady Grace fan

Most Privy and Secrete

The Daybooke of my Lady Grace Cavendish,
Maid of Honour to Her Gracious Majesty
Queen Elizabeth I of that name

At Her Majesty's Palace Hampton Court,
upon the River Thames, Surrey

The Twenty-fifth Day of September, in the Year of Our Lord 1570

In my bedchamber early evening

We arrived at Hampton Court Palace just this morning and already something terrible has happened. I had been very much looking forward to our stay; but within hours of stepping off the Royal Barge, I was presented with a new mystery to solve.

And solve it I must, for I am the Queen's secret Lady Pursuivant, seeking out any and all wrongdoers who would trouble Her Majesty's peace.

I think I shall have time to write down what has happened in my daybooke, for Mary Shelton and Lady Sarah Bartelmy are still dressing for supper. Lady Sarah is nowhere near dressed and cannot decide which sleeves to wear with her new stomacher – a beautiful white satin one that has golden bone lace running down the middle. It was given to her by her loyal suitor, Daniel Cheshire, and even I have to admit that he has excellent taste – for a gentleman. Poor Olwen has all Sarah's sleeves laid out on her bed, while my lady scrutinizes each of them.

I am proud to say that I am nowhere near as troubling for my tiring woman. The only reason I am not ready for dinner is because my skirt has a very slight flaw from when I caught it on a nail and tore off some of the seed pearls. I barely noticed it myself, but my dear Ellie Bunting will not let me attend the Queen until it is mended.

I am still a little shocked at what has taken place at Court today, and so is everyone else. I will write it all down from the beginning. It will help pass the time while Ellie fusses over my skirts.

Hampton Court has always been one of my favourite palaces to visit, because there are wonderful trees in the parkland. I used to climb them when I was younger and not so likely to be reprimanded for such behaviour. When the Queen told Secretary Cecil that she desired to see if her Surrey palace played host to autumn colours yet, I decided there and then that I would do what I

could to sneak away and find a good tree to climb!

I whispered my intent to Ellie as we sat together on the Royal Barge this morning.

'God save us, Grace,' she hissed. 'What about the mess you'll make of your clothes? You're not a child any more!'

That was rich, for she is younger than me. Since becoming my tiring woman Ellie has grown fussier about proper behaviour than Mrs Champernowne, the Mistress of the Maids!

I squeezed her arm and said coaxingly, '*You* love to climb trees as much as I do.'

A look of longing came over her face. 'Well,' she muttered, trying to remain stern, 'if you're so determined, then I should be there to keep an eye on you. If that means I've got to do a bit of climbing too, then so be it.'

But I am straying from my tale. I must arrange my thoughts and record exactly what happened. We arrived here in the mid-morning, with the usual harbingers and trumpets and all manner of boring ceremony. When Lord Howard, who looks after Hampton Court for the Queen, had finished his speechifying, Mrs Champernowne spoke with Her Majesty and then bustled across the Presence Chamber towards us Maids. She flapped her hands

as she always does when she is about to herd the Maids of Honour anywhere.

'Now, girls, make haste, for you are to have a huge treat,' she said. 'With Michaelmas nearly upon us, the Queen wishes you all to practise your dancing. You are to have lessons every day with Monsieur Danton, look you – and he awaits you now in the Great Hall!'

My heart sank to my boots. Dancing is all very well for those who want to flirt and compete for the attentions of the young men at Court. As I do not have any wish to marry and leave Her Majesty's side, there seems to be no point to it at all. I would sooner spend a whole day doing Latin translations. But I knew the Queen loved Michaelmas, especially the dancing, and I was prepared to suffer for Her Majesty's pleasure.

Unlike me, Lady Jane Coningsby and Lady Sarah are most keen on dancing – although now that Sarah has her faithful Gentleman of the Guard, Daniel, she may not wish to vie with Jane so much. I shall miss the fun if those two ladies are no longer at loggerheads over eligible gentlemen!

Anyway, I think I must have groaned out loud – or else Our Gracious Queen is a mind reader – for she caught my eye and announced, without a

flicker of a smile, that she would have her dogs walked immediately.

'Has no one given a thought to poor Henri or Philip or Ivan?' she said sternly. 'They have been imprisoned in their baskets for the whole journey from Richmond Palace and must needs stretch their little legs.' Her glance alighted, as if by chance, on me. 'Lady Grace, you will tend to the poor creatures and forgo your dancing lesson. Go and do my bidding without delay!'

I arranged my face in a disappointed frown and curtsied backwards out of the Presence Chamber. Then I ran to my bedchamber.

The Queen truly is the most wonderful godmother anyone could have in the whole wide world – when she is not in a temper and throwing things, that is. She has been like a mother to me ever since my own mother died saving her life, and probably knows me better than anyone else.

In my bedchamber, I found Ellie fussing over some imagined blemish on a stomacher. I quickly changed into an old kirtle and we were soon out in the fresh air of Middle Park, with the Queen's dogs straining at their leashes. They were delighted when we set them free, and raced to every tree in the area.

While the dogs had their fun, I decided to have mine own. I led Ellie to an ancient oak tree with low branches in a secluded corner of Middle Park. It is one I have been climbing ever since I was old enough to pull myself up into it. Ellie and I scrambled as high as we could. It was a marvellous feeling, looking down over the palace and the sparkling river beyond and knowing that no one could see us! I hoped Ellie wouldn't scold me later, for I got a green smear all down one sleeve.

'It is a pity Masou is so often busy at his tumbling practice,' I exclaimed as we sat together on a broad branch and swung our legs. 'He would love this!'

'Wouldn't he show off!' answered Ellie, picking an acorn and using its shell to make a hat for her finger. 'He'd 'ave shinned up each tree in the park by turns while we were still at the first!'

I laughed. 'True. And then hung upside-down like a monkey and teased us for our clumsy climbing.'

'And reminded us that he's the best tumbler in England.'

'Do not forget, Ellie,' I said with mock seriousness, 'that before he came to this country, he was the best tumbler in the whole of Africa.'

We were interrupted by one of the dogs growling below us. I looked down to see the back end of Ivan sticking out of a rabbit hole. The sight was so funny we both burst out laughing – until we realized that we would have to do something about it!

'Make haste, Ellie,' I spluttered, nearly falling in my hurry to climb down. 'We shall never find him if he goes underground. Imagine what the Queen will say!'

'But you have to own he does look right comical.' Ellie chortled as she followed.

We reached the ground just in time to grab Ivan's disappearing bum and pull him out of the hole. He looked most cross at being thwarted, and seemed to get even angrier when we carried on laughing. We gathered up Henri and Philip – who did not want to be caught, either – and coaxed all three of them back towards the palace, past the buildings where the craftsmen work. I suppose Ivan's blood was up, for he strained and pulled at his leash, nearly taking me off my feet. As I stumbled, his lead slipped from my hand and he went scampering off through an open doorway. Philip and Henri barked furiously and practically choked as they tried to follow him, but luckily

Ellie had their leashes tightly in her hand. I did not want to imagine what Her Majesty would say if Ivan came out covered in paint and wood shavings! There was nothing for it but to tie the others to a tree and give chase.

We both ran to the door we had seen him enter and found ourselves in a dingy passageway.

'I don't see him,' said Ellie, panting.

'Here, Ivan!' I called coaxingly. When he didn't return, I tried my best impression of Her Majesty, hoping he would respond to authority: 'Come to Grace! Now!'

I hoped to hear the patter of claws on the flagstones, but instead a terrible cry came from further down the passage.

'Hell's teeth!' muttered Ellie as we made our way towards the sound. 'What's that pesky dog done now?'

We turned the corner and came to an open door. I knew this place. It was the workshop of Mr Urseau, the clockmaker. I had come here once before with my mother when I was very young. I remembered it well, for the room had been full of clocks of all shapes and sizes, which were most fascinating.

I was expecting to see a naughty Ivan being

chastised by the clockmaker and so it took my brain a few seconds to register the horror of the sight before us. Mr Urseau was lying on his back on the floor. A dagger protruded from his chest, and his clothes were soaked with blood, which had started to pool on the floor around him. A skinny young man was kneeling by him, clutching at his sleeve. It took me a moment to notice that poor Ivan was cowering in a far corner, whimpering at the dreadful sight to which he had led us.

'God preserve us!' wailed Ellie, and she tried to push me away from the door. 'Get away from here, Grace.' She looked all around her with wide, frightened eyes. 'You could be in danger.'

There was no time to tell her that I would not be much of a Lady Pursuivant if I fled the scene of a mystery. I stepped into the room towards the frightened dog and pulled Ellie behind me.

'Put Ivan on his leash, Ellie,' I said quietly. 'Else he will just get in the way.' She gawped at me as if I were speaking Scottish. 'Go on!' I repeated.

Creeping round the very edge of the room, she did as I asked. The young man was now grasping poor Mr Urseau by the shoulders.

'Master,' he implored. I could hear that his voice had a slight foreign accent. 'It is Charles. Tell me who did this. Open your eyes, I beg of you.'

I could not believe what happened next. Even though he had a dagger deep in his chest, Mr Urseau's eyelids fluttered. Somehow, he was still alive! He stared up at the young man and moved his lips as if he would speak, but he could only make a horrible gurgling sound in his throat. The memory of it now makes me shudder.

The young man held the poor stricken clockmaker's head as if to cradle him. 'What was that, Master?' he asked. 'What are you trying to say?'

I found myself holding my breath. Was Mr Urseau about to name his attacker? I bent closer to hear his last words. Even though I was in the corner of the room, I am sure I heard them aright, but I still cannot think what he meant by them.

'The Queen,' he whispered. Then his eyes dulled and his body went limp. Mr Urseau was dead.

Charles howled in anguish and almost collapsed over the body of his master, rocking and holding him as if he would bring him back to life.

'Murder!'

I jumped and turned round at the sound of a hostile voice. A burly man wearing a dusty apron had burst into the room. I knew him to be one of the palace carpenters. With a grunt, he hauled the whimpering apprentice to his feet and held him tight in one muscled arm.

'No use trying to escape!' he growled as Charles struggled and protested his innocence in whimpering sobs.

Other workmen were pouring into the room now and no one had taken any notice of Ellie and me in the corner.

'There's been a foul murder, and here's the villain who did it,' shouted the carpenter. 'I caught him at the deed, treacherous Dutchman. See how he's covered in poor Nick's blood.'

'Aye, that's clear enough,' called someone in the crowd.

'He should get the same treatment,' growled another.

'Murderer!'

Several people took up the chant as Charles was pushed into the middle of the throng. He stood trembling and shaking his head.

I felt sorry for him, but it did seem very likely that he was guilty, for we had found him next to the body only moments after hearing Mr Urseau's cry of pain. Charles had been the only other person in the room, and Ellie and I had not seen anyone else leaving the workshop. Still, the agony I'd seen on his face when Mr Urseau died made it impossible for me to leave him in the hands of these angry workmen.

I spotted a young servant boy who was jumping in the air, trying look over the heads of the men so he could see the body.

I stepped out of the shadows and tapped him on the shoulder. 'You!' I said, again adopting a voice rather like the Queen's, to assert my authority. 'Fetch the Captain of the Queen's Guard on the instant.'

The boy jumped in surprise and everyone turned to look at me. There was a moment of stunned silence. A Maid of Honour and her tiring woman were obviously the last people the workmen expected to see. As one, they bowed and shuffled their feet anxiously.

'Begging your pardon, my lady,' said the carpenter who had grabbed hold of Charles. 'I didn't see you there.'

'That is no matter,' I replied firmly. I turned to the gawping servant boy. 'Make haste now and fetch Mr Hatton.'

The boy ran.

The crowd stood awkwardly in the room as we waited. I took the time to study the suspect,

Charles. I have to say he was a soft, mawkish young man who did not look capable of stabbing anyone!

He began to gabble into the silence. 'I am innocent,' he said between sobs. 'I heard Mr Urseau cry out from down the passageway and tried to get to him . . . But I fumbled with my key and could not get the door unlocked in time.' He stared down at his hands. 'Curse these useless fingers!' He twisted his head to look down at the lifeless body. 'How will I manage without you?' he wailed. 'You taught me everything I know.'

Something did not sit right with me. Charles was heartbroken at the loss of his master. Either that or he was a very fine actor indeed. I was starting to suspect that the facts were perhaps not as plain as they appeared.

Charles said that he could not unlock the door, which meant it must have been locked when he arrived. But, if the murderer was not Charles, then the villain had done the deed in great haste and run off very swiftly and I doubted whether he would have had time to stop and lock the door behind him! Workmen had soon poured into Mr Urseau's workshop from all sides, and surely Ellie and I would have seen someone fleeing via the corridors.

'We should string the Dutchman up!' shouted a voice.

'Aye, hang the villain,' another joined in.

Charles cowered in fear as the workmen jostled forward. The carpenter stood over him threateningly – his strong, bare arms looked as if they could snap the poor man in half.

'This is no place for a Maid of Honour,' he said, turning to me. I wondered whether these men would have already meted out their own justice if I had not been there!

But I was determined to stay. 'Royal protocol,' I told them, 'decrees that no one is to leave this room until Mr Hatton has come and spoken to all the witnesses.' I stepped towards Charles. 'Whatever this man has done, he will have to answer to the Captain of Her Majesty's Guard. Mr Hatton will not thank anyone who has frightened him out of his wits.'

My words seemed to calm the crowd down.

'Now, Charles,' I said soothingly, 'Mr Hatton will ask you many questions about this murder – and he will expect straight answers. He may want to know' – I pretended to hesitate – 'why the workshop door was locked when Mr Urseau was inside.'

'It is always locked, my lady,' said Charles, bowing anxiously at me, 'whether we are inside or out. The clocks and watches in here are too precious to let some knave carry them off.'

'Pot calling the kettle black,' muttered a voice at the back of the crowd.

'And who else has a key to the workshop?' I went on, ignoring the murmurs of agreement from the men.

'Only Mr Urseau and myself,' said the apprentice, looking gratefully at me. He must have been relieved to find someone who was determined to keep him safe from the crowd. 'Mine is in the door still, and see' – he gestured towards a hook where a single key hung – 'my master's is in its usual place on the wall.'

'And has no one else a key?' I asked.

Charles shook his head. 'Only the two of us work in here, my lady,' he explained. 'There is no need for more keys.'

Looking around, I could see that the three workshop windows were not the kind that would open and that the glass was intact. The chimney had a fire in it, so that would not provide a way out. There was a grilled grate in the chimneybreast, but that was for ventilation only and firmly plastered into the brickwork. There seemed to be no other means of leaving the chamber.

I frowned. 'Then how could the murderer have got out?'

The apprentice sagged. 'I know not, my lady,' he said. 'I saw no one fleeing. I understand how one might think me guilty . . . but I swear I did not kill my dear master. And I cannot think of anyone who would want to murder such a good man.'

'This is all fibble-fabble, Charles Doute!' exclaimed the carpenter, red in the face. He strode around the room, flinging open cupboard doors. 'If what you say is true, then the villain is still in this very room with us and I shall find him – for he did not leave by either the door or the windows. Mayhap he was a magician who locked the door behind him and then put the key back on the hook inside!'

All the cupboard doors were open now, and we could see that there was nothing but tools and clock workings on the shelves inside. None of them were big enough for a man to hide in. 'No one here at all.' He strode up to Charles and put his face right up to the trembling apprentice's. 'It was you, boy. You murdered your master for his position, and in cold blood too.'

Ellie pulled at my sleeve anxiously.

I coughed loudly. The carpenter remembered himself and reluctantly stepped back.

'Can you recall what you were doing when you heard your master's cry?' I asked Charles. 'Mr Hatton is sure to need to know.'

'That I can,' answered Charles. 'I was coming to start my day, after breaking my fast in the kitchens. I was just down the passageway when I heard the . . . terrible sound . . . and at first I did not think it could have come from inside the workshop.'

'Why?' I asked.

'Because last night Mr Urseau told me he would not be at his work this morning. He said he had a meeting to go to late last night and would need to catch up on his sleep.'

The mention of a meeting took my interest. It could have some bearing on the crime. 'And did he tell you the reason he had to go to the meeting?'

'Oh no, my lady,' said Charles. 'He often had such meetings, but they were usually at night, and most secret. I knew nothing about them, and I wouldn't ask. It wouldn't have been right.'

I thought these secret meetings could have much significance, but I could not pry too closely as I might raise the workmen's suspicions about my curiosity.

However, I thought I might learn more by examining the body. I looked down at Charles's dead master, the dagger still lodged in his chest. It was of course possible that the clockmaker had taken his own life, but I did not think so. The dagger was thrust in to the hilt and Mr Urseau would not have had the strength to drive so deep into his own body.

The clockmaker's arms lay beside his body, and now I spotted something clutched in one hand. It looked like a small key. Could that be significant? I wondered. I drew Ellie's attention to it with a subtle nudge. My poor tiring woman followed my gaze, shielding her eyes from the blood. She looked back at me, and I could tell that she too thought the key significant.

While Charles continued to protest his innocence, I drew my friend to the door and made a pretence of looking out for Mr Hatton's arrival.

'This is a most strange and puzzling affair,' I whispered to her. 'We must discover exactly how Mr Urseau came to be murdered.'

Ellie almost snorted her reply. 'It's not strange or puzzling, really,' she said. 'We happened upon a murderer and his victim in the same room – and no one else around. I reckon *I* should be the Lady Pursuivant if you can't work that one out!'

'But Charles may be innocent, Ellie,' I insisted in a low voice. 'He seems truly distressed about what has happened, and surely if he were the murderer, he would try to cover his tracks a little. He would say that he saw someone running away – or that the door was already open when he arrived. Something that would make us doubt his guilt.'

'But, Grace, think on it,' urged Ellie. 'We saw no one leaving here, so if it wasn't Charles, then the villain must have walked right through the wall! Unless Mr Urseau was killed by a ghost, there is no mystery to investigate. So don't let that head of yours go running places it shouldn't be running. That way lies only trouble.'

'My dear Ellie,' I said, 'you would not have a man accused if he might be innocent, would you?'

'Course not!' exclaimed Ellie. 'That'd be wrong. And I know better than most what it's like to be locked up for something you haven't done.' Her face clouded with sadness for a moment. This past winter, she had been wrongfully arrested by Her Majesty's Guards for a theft she had not committed. The matter was eventually resolved, and

Ellie was exonerated, but the memory of her time locked up in prison clearly still upset her.

'Do you really think it might be someone else?' she asked.

'I do not know yet,' I said. 'I know it may sound strange, but there is something in Charles that makes me doubt his guilt. I must think further on the matter. Those secret meetings and the key in his hand . . . And Mr Urseau's last words were "the Queen". That could be important as well.'

' "The Queen"?' whispered Ellie. 'I think your ears are stoppered, Grace. Mr Urseau didn't say "the Queen". He said "the key". I heard that most clearly. Anyway, why would he say "the Queen"?'

'I confess I do not know,' I answered. 'Unless he was showing his loyalty to his Sovereign with his dying breath.'

I must add here what a fine thing that would be. I hope I could be as noble in such circumstances.

'But I am sure he said "the Queen",' I insisted.

Ellie shook her head. 'It was definitely "the key".'

Perhaps Ellie was right, but now was not the time to argue. 'I want to find out about those meetings. Could they be something to do with Her Majesty?' I asked her.

'Not if he said "the key",' muttered Ellie doggedly.

I did not have time to make any answer as Mr Christopher Hatton and two of his Gentlemen Guards came striding down the passageway towards us. I dragged Ellie back behind the door. I knew that, if he saw me, Hatton would order me away without hesitation – for my own safety, he would doubtless say.

The Captain of the Queen's Guard burst into the workshop, followed by his men, their swords drawn. The carpenter was quick to tell his version of events – with an amendment making himself the first to find the victim – and gave his decided opinion of the matter.

'Seize the wretch!' barked Mr Hatton, once the carpenter had told his tale. The two guards wasted no time in taking hold of Charles, who put up no resistance, but hung in their grasp as if he had not an ounce of strength left. They dragged him towards the door. Unless I acted quickly I might miss the opportunity to tell Mr Hatton what I knew. Her Majesty's loyal Captain of the Guard thinks of me as nothing but a meddling Maid – I admit I might have popped up and got in the way of his investigations once or twice in the past. However, were it not for my help, I do believe that half the villains that have troubled the Court would still be running about.

I pushed through the crowd and stood before him. I saw him start as he set eyes on me, but I did not give him a chance to speak.

'Mr Hatton,' I said quickly, ignoring his frown, 'I believe I may be able to help—'

'I doubt it, Lady Grace,' replied the Captain of the Guard with a stiff bow. 'Maids of Honour and murders do not sit well together.' (If only he knew!) 'Now, please excuse me—'

I stood my ground. 'I was merely going to say that I may be able to save you time in your investigation. I know how busy you are about the Queen's business. I was the first to reach the terrible scene after Charles Doute, and am happy to tell you all I saw. That way, the truth of the matter will be out the sooner.'

Mr Hatton's expression changed immediately. 'Of course, Lady Grace. What exactly did you see?' He gave a suspicious glance at the carpenter, whose version of events now seemed to be in doubt. The man shuffled his feet in embarrassment.

Beginning my tale with Ivan's escape and our excuse for being in the room, I explained exactly what Ellie and I had witnessed. And I left one thing until last, hoping that Mr Hatton would take special note of it.

'Mr Urseau was desperate to tell us something before he died,' I said. 'His last words were "the Queen".'

Ellie humphed and Mr Hatton turned his gaze on her. 'I suppose you have something to add?' he asked with one eyebrow raised. Normally, someone like Ellie would be well beneath the notice of such a man.

'Begging your pardon, sir,' she said, 'but I heard "the key", not "the Queen".' She pointed to Mr Urseau's dead clenched fist. 'Perhaps he meant the one he's holding.'

Mr Hatton glared at her. He obviously did not approve of a tiring woman pointing out evidence to him. Though I disagreed with Ellie's version of the clockmaker's last words, I still had to hide my smile. Since she had been promoted to my tiring woman, dear Ellie had become much more bold in dealing with her superiors.

Nevertheless, Mr Hatton did bend over the body and gather up the key with as much dignity as he could muster. This was not very easy, for he had to pick his way over the pool of blood. At last he held it up. The key was small and silver.

Mr Hatton whirled round to Charles and held up the key menacingly. 'Tell me what this key is for,' he commanded.

'I–I don't know,' Charles stuttered, but it was clear that Mr Hatton did not believe him.

'It is certainly not the key to this workshop,' he said, putting it in the pouch on his belt. 'I will find out where it comes from later,' he added, looking sharply at Charles. 'It may help to explain this wretch's motive. Men, take him away.'

Charles Doute was dragged off, whimpering.

How timely! Ellie has fixed my skirt, and now I hear Mrs Champernowne calling us all to supper. I believe I have recorded everything I need to, but this morning has left me much to think on.

That night, after supper

I am writing this in my chamber. Ellie is combing my hair, which is very soothing – even though she is complaining that she keeps finding bits of tree in my locks! This is hard to believe after the brushing she gave it before supper! I am fortunate in having a good candle with no hint of a splutter – I will need plenty of light to record all that has happened today.

I took my seat at supper and was not surprised to find rumours buzzing about the Great Hall like bees in a hive. It is always thus with a mystery at Court.

I was sitting with a Maid on either side of me – Lucy Throckmorton and Lady Jane. Across the table was Samuel Twyer, one of the Gentlemen Guard.

'That villain Charles is in the Hampton village lock-up,' he told us with relish. 'And that's too good for him.'

Lucy nodded. 'I agree.' She was holding a chicken leg and waggled it at him to emphasize her point. 'Indeed, I am certain I know the motive for his foul deed.' She looked around at us all. 'He murdered his master because he wanted to be master himself. It is obvious. Mr Charles Doute wished to be the Royal Clockmaker.'

Round the table people were nodding their agreement, but I was loath to point the finger. It is my duty as Lady Pursuivant to investigate and determine Charles's guilt or innocence for sure. And of course, if I find him innocent, then I have a murderer to track down. And a very skilled and clever one too.

At that moment Lady Jane took my sleeve. 'Do you not find the hare delicious?' she asked me in a rush, poking at the meat on her plate with her knife. 'I believe the sauce to be made from pomegranates.'

Normally I would have been surprised to find Lady Jane making conversation with me when she has a gentleman on her other side. Especially one as handsome as Sir Thomas Cartwright, who seemed most keen to flirt with her. And I have never known Jane to be interested in recipes before!

However, I knew full well why she was turning her back on that particular gentleman. Sir Thomas might be tall, with dark glossy hair and piercing blue eyes, but he has not been careful with his friends. He is acquainted with the Earl of Northumberland, who – with the Earl of Westmoreland – led a rebellion against the Queen last year. They wished to bring England back into the Catholic religion and, much worse, put Mary, who was Queen of Scotland, on the throne instead of Her Majesty. The rebellion failed of course, for most are loyal to Queen Elizabeth, and the two earls fled the country to avoid torture and the executioner's block. Now anyone who is friendly with the northern earls is looked upon with distrust.

Before the unsuccessful rebellion, Sir Thomas was very popular at Court, particularly with my fine lady. But now his name is tainted with suspicion, and he has been trying most fervently to curry favour with those close to the Queen. He obviously had hopes that Lady Jane would look kindly on him, but she was unyielding in her desire to discuss pomegranate sauce with me.

Sir Thomas tried his hardest to attract her attention again as we made our way from the Great Hall to the Banqueting House for our dessert. He bowed deeply before her.

'May I escort you, my lady?' he simpered. 'Though nothing on the table will compare to the sweetness of your smile.'

Jane glared at him with no trace of a smile, sweet or otherwise. 'Oh, Grace,' she exclaimed in a false, bright tone as she pointed through the open door of the Banqueting House. 'Look at those plum pies. The pastry is so . . . shiny. I must have one at once.' And, sweeping around the still bending Sir Thomas, she marched me off to the shiny pies.

However, Sir Thomas did not give up. As we returned to the Great Hall for the evening's entertainment, I saw him hovering. Jane must have seen him too, for she grasped my arm even tighter.

'Come, Grace,' she ordered me, holding up her skirts with her free hand. 'The Queen has need of us.'

But the Queen had not required us all evening. Mrs Champernowne looked most displeased as we hurried past her and almost caught up with Her Majesty.

The Great Hall had been swept and cleared in preparation for an entertainment by Mr Somers's troupe. Jane sat us down firmly between Sir Pelham Poucher and Lady Sarah. Lady Sarah had Mr Cheshire on her other side, and not even a horse could get past the portly Sir Pelham, so we were safe from Sir Thomas's unwanted attentions. Sarah seemed content to sit next to Jane, and since she met her precious Daniel, she can hardly be bothered to throw insults Jane's way.

Jane, for her part, seemed unaware that her hated

rival was sitting right beside her, and chatted away to me as if she had not a care in the world – although I noticed her eyes darting anxiously around every now and then to see where her would-be suitor was. Usually she does not have much to say to me, but tonight I was very glad she chose me as her shield, for the conversation quickly took an interesting turn.

'Of course, Lucy has it wrong,' she said suddenly.

'Has what wrong?' I asked, peering over at Lucy, who was deep in a conversation about sleeves with Carmina Willoughby. Although Lucy is new to the Court, the two Maids have become close friends.

'The motive for the murder!' declared Jane.

This was much more interesting than discussing the fullness of sleeves. 'Why do *you* think Mr Urseau was killed?' I said.

'Not for Charles Doute to become Royal Clockmaker, that is for sure.' Jane began to look around the room again and I thought she would say no more.

'Then why?' I nudged her arm.

'For Mr Urseau's treasure!' Jane explained. 'He was known as a man who was careful with money and never seemed to have much to spend. His wife certainly complained about him being a miser. But, secretly, the man was hoarding his wealth. He had a veritable pile of gold.'

'How do you know this?' I asked, amazed.

'Well . . . I do not know it for sure,' Jane admitted. 'But we all heard that he clutched a key in his hand when he died, and of course that must be the key to his treasure chest. Even in dying he tried to hold onto it.'

This was very interesting. Gossip, to be sure – but often tittle-tattle begins with the truth. I was about to ask her if she knew any more when we were interrupted by a voice behind us.

'It has been a sad day for us all, losing such a craftsman as Mr Urseau.'

We both jumped and turned to find Sir Thomas sitting behind us. I wanted to curse him for interrupting Jane just when she was about to tell me something important. But before we could turn away, he quickly went on.

'We had much in common, you see,' he said sadly. 'We both shared a love of clocks.'

It would have been too rude to ignore him now. Jane seemed dumbstruck by his persistence, so I nodded politely.

'And watches . . .' Sir Thomas put his hands to a chain around his neck, lifting it up to show us. A beautiful watch hung from it. It was about four inches across and resembled a flat drum. The brass cover was intricately engraved with a hunting scene. He opened the lid to show us the face with its Roman numerals. 'This is the latest addition to my collection.' His words were aimed at Lady Jane but I was interested in spite of myself. 'It comes from Germany, where the finest watches are made,' Sir Thomas went on, stroking the engraved cover. 'Look at the fine chiselling and piercing. I was hoping to show it to Mr Urseau, God rest his soul.' He sighed sadly, but then brightened a little. 'Perhaps you would like to inspect it, Lady Jane, for I am sure you would appreciate such a fine thing, being so beautiful yourself.'

I could see a struggle going on inside Jane's head and it was all I could do not to laugh out loud. On the one hand, Sir Thomas was to be kept at a distance because of his dubious friendships. On the other, he was actually a fine suitor for Jane to encourage – being handsome and obviously very rich, if this watch was an example of his possessions. Watches are not common at Court – the Queen has the only collection that I know of. Sir Thomas's must have cost him a fortune. I wondered which way Jane would go but I did not have to wonder long. She suddenly put her hand up to her face and fluttered her eyelashes frantically.

'Faith!' she exclaimed. 'I cannot look at anything. I have something in my eye.' And she turned away and resolutely kept her gaze facing forward, dabbing at her eye with a handkerchief.

I was about to prompt Jane continue her tale of the treasure when I was interrupted by yet another young man! This time he was heralded by a roll of drums – Masou had made his appearance in the Great Hall. He sped across the floor in a series of somersaults, each higher than the one before. It was breathtaking – though I would never tell him so, lest his head grow to the size of the palace itself. He was quickly followed by the rest of Mr Somers's troupe, tumbling, juggling and eating fire! That was French Louis' part in the display. I knew I would get no more from Jane now and resigned myself to enjoying the spectacle, which was not hard. But I did worry that French Louis might set his beard alight.

Although we had taken seats, it became clear that the entertainment was to be all over the hall. I saw the Queen rise and walk among the acrobats, which gave the rest of us leave to do the same. I was delighted. I always look for a chance to talk with Masou and he was going to be especially useful tonight. Rumours and gossip are not restricted to courtiers – many's the time I have learned something useful from what my tumbling friend has heard from the servants. I sauntered over to where Masou was standing on his hands and tried to look as if I were merely watching. But something must have made him notice me, for he quickly jumped to his feet, shoved his hands into his pockets and produced four oranges. He bowed to the applause of the people around and then began to juggle the oranges high into the air.

'You have something of great import to impart,' he said to me from the corner of his mouth.

'How did you know that?' I gasped.

He grinned. 'I saw the impatient tap of your slipper when I was upside-down,' he said. 'Let me guess. You have news about the weather, or plum tartlets or . . . mayhap the dreadful murder of the esteemed Royal Clockmaker.'

'Well, of course you are right,' I said impatiently. 'Tell me, have you heard anything? Lucy Throckmorton says Charles Doute wanted to be Clockmaker and got rid of Mr Urseau to be sure of it. But Lady Jane says Charles desired his master's treasure. One thing is certain: all seem sure that the apprentice did the deed.'

Masou suddenly tossed an orange to me! This was clever. If I was involved in his trick, we could be seen conversing at our leisure and no one would guess it was not simply part of his acrobatic banter. I was also glad that I caught it cleanly and did not make a fool of myself.

'I knew you would investigate the murder,' he said. 'And I agree with your doubt about Charles. I know him but a little, yet I think him devoted to his master. Others may know different. I shall keep my ears open for you, my lady.'

He collected his oranges, threw one to a surprised Mrs Champernowne and then cartwheeled off!

Little Gypsy Pete stopped in front of me, threw himself down and began a series of forward rolls. I clapped and smiled at him – at least, I *think* I did, for my mind was busy with curiosity.

As I pretended to watch the troupe, I let my head collect together everything that I had learned so far. If treasure were involved, then there might be no mystery at all. Money has often proved a motive for murder in my past investigations. Charles Doute had worked closely with Mr Urseau and would be sure to know how wealthy his master was.

As I thought back to the terrible scene in the workshop earlier in the day, three things troubled my mind enough to convince me that this was not a simple case of greed begetting murder.

Firstly, there was the matter of Mr Urseau's dying words. I firmly believed he had said 'the Queen', which had nothing to do with treasure. I was also certain he'd spoken these words to Charles. Surely he would not have said anything like that to a man who had just stuck a dagger in his chest. The clockmaker would have been more likely to gasp out the word 'murderer'!

Secondly, what had Charles meant by the 'secret meetings' that his master attended? Did they fit into this puzzle somehow? If Mr Urseau truly had been at a meeting late last night, what had he been doing in the workshop so early this morning? After all, he had told Charles he would be sleeping in.

The third thing that bothered me was that I felt Charles had been telling the truth. Although it seemed he had been caught red-handed, I had seen enough mysteries to know that the obvious solution was not always the right one. If Charles was not the murderer, then Mr Urseau had been stabbed to death while apparently alone in his workshop, with only a locked door as a means of escape. How could that be possible? The only way it could have been done was if the knave were a phantom with a talent for slipping through walls! And that was just too fanciful an idea for me to take seriously.

I decided I must see the Queen about the matter. We had not had a chance to talk about it. I made my way through the throngs of laughing courtiers and stood by her side. She was watching French Louis perform his fire-eating. Secretary Cecil and Robert Dudley, Earl of Leicester, were watching her. I believe they were anxious that Her Majesty was too close to the flame, but neither would have dared tell her so.

I curtsied deeply.

'Lady Grace,' said the Queen, 'do you not wonder how Louis does this trick? Methinks he will need much small beer to cool his throat.'

I smiled at her joke. 'It is quite a spectacle.'

She took my chin in her hand and stared into my eyes for a moment. 'Walk with me,' she ordered. 'I have not forgotten that you were witness to a terrible scene today.'

People bowed as we crossed the floor and walked out into the passageway. We were alone here apart from two members of her Guard who came along behind.

'Have Mrs Champernowne make you a posset to help you sleep tonight,' said the Queen. 'And you will soon forget what you saw.'

I nodded. 'It does trouble me, Your Majesty.' I wanted to tell her that I had no intention of forgetting anything about the murder, but I could not contradict her. I tried to find the right words.

'My Liege,' I began, 'I do not believe that Charles Doute killed his master.'

The Queen stopped and an impatient look came over her face. 'Mr Hatton has told me the facts and Charles Doute is the only one who could have done it. I will not have you seeing mysteries where there are none to be seen.'

I opened my mouth to protest, but the Queen cut me off. 'Perhaps you do not have enough to occupy yourself. I have an excellent notion on how to remedy that. We have received a fifteen-page letter from the French Ambassador. It is in French, of course, but you could translate it into Latin for me!'

I wonder if my face went as white as it felt! I curtsied deeply and muttered that I must find Mrs Champernowne and ask her for that posset. The Queen waved me away and I fled!

And now to bed. I am not the only one to be distracted by this mystery. Ellie paused more than once in her combing as she pondered it all. One of her ponderings was very useful.

'You won't believe what Jem Ainsworth has been saying, Grace.'

I had no idea who she was talking about and told her so.

'You know, that fat porter who's always round the kitchens after food. Well, I heard he's been bragging that he was the last one to see Mr Urseau alive! Liar! He wasn't anywhere near that workshop. We wouldn't have missed him – he's so large.'

'Why would he claim such a thing?' I wondered.

'Seems he did see him earlier on the day he died,' said Ellie. 'Least that's what I heard.'

This might just be idle gossip, I suppose, but it could be true. In which case Jem Ainsworth could have some useful information.

I have three tasks to take me forward in this investigation.

1. Seek out the porter.
2. Find out whether Mr Urseau had some treasure.
3. Discover the reason for the 'secret meetings'.

The Twenty-sixth Day of September, in the Year of Our Lord 1570

Early afternoon

I am sitting under a tree in the Privy Orchard. The sun is warm today and I am glad of the shade. We have had our noontide meal and my full belly and the sunshine would be sure to send me to sleep! Although the noise from the nearby kitchens may help to keep me awake.

Last night I tossed and turned on my pillow, thinking about the mystery. My thoughts troubled me so that I overslept. Indeed, when I awoke, Lady Sarah was up and dressed. I felt most slothful as I dragged myself out of bed.

Perhaps it is as well that I have had some extra sleep, for I have an exciting night ahead.

After breakfast, I set about my investigations as soon as I could. Mrs Champernowne was rushing about like a sheepdog to get the Maids to another dancing lesson. I wanted the time to look into this terrible crime, and so, when she had delivered us, I told Monsieur Danton I thought I had a cold coming. To prove the point, I brought forth a tremendous sneeze.

'*Mon Dieu!*' he shrieked, flapping his hands at me. 'Get away.' Then he hastily guided me to the entrance of the Great Hall, chasing me out with his handkerchief. I knew that sneezing would do the trick. Monsieur Danton has a fear of illness and suchlike. I have heard that once, when he pricked his finger on a rose thorn, he fainted at the sight of the tiny drop of blood.

I found Ellie and we set off to look for Jem Ainsworth. I wanted to hear about his meeting with Mr Urseau for myself. We went to the Privy Kitchen and struck lucky, for he was skulking around waiting to see what titbits had been left from the Court's breakfast.

'He does not seem in great need of extra food,' I whispered to Ellie. 'He is as well covered as Sir Pelham Poucher!'

Ellie gave a snort of laughter. We were just making our way over to the porter when I heard Mrs Champernowne's voice. I dived down behind a table of plucked chickens, pulling Ellie with me. I could not let the Mistress of the Maids see me in the kitchen when I was supposed to be at my dancing lesson!

'I need a posset for poor Lady Anne,' she was saying. 'Her throat is raw. I will supervise the making of it myself.'

'Oh no,' I groaned softly. 'She will be here an age, fussing over the boiling of the milk and whatnot. We are trapped.'

Ellie tugged at my sleeve and pointed behind us. There was a small door leading out to another passageway. We crawled across the floor to it, making the poor spitboy jump in surprise.

Outside we straightened our clothes and tried to look innocent. Mr Friar, the head cook, was sitting in a room nearby doing his accounts. He gave us a quizzical glance.

'We will leave Jem to another time,' I said to Ellie. 'He is sure to be back in the kitchen before long. Let us make a visit to the clockmaker's widow, to see what she has to say about her husband having any treasure. She may also know something of the secret meetings of which Charles spoke. I am sure they are important.'

And if Mrs Champernowne came to hear that I had not been at the dancing lesson, she could not complain – for I was making a compassionate visit to a bereaved woman.

We went out through the orchard and across the moat to reach the row of cottages where Mrs Urseau lived.

I lifted the heavy knocker, wondering if the grieving widow would welcome visitors. Before I could knock a second time, the door was flung open by a young woman in a black shawl.

I was surprised that this was Mr Urseau's wife. She was much younger than him – and rather fair, to boot. I suppose I must have been staring, for the woman looked at me and frowned.

'May I help you?' she said abruptly.

'Mrs Urseau?' I asked. The woman nodded. 'I am Lady Grace Cavendish, Maid of Honour to Her Majesty. I am here to offer you my deepest sympathies.'

The clockmaker's widow remembered her manners and made a brief curtsy. Then she stood aside and waved us into a small, dark room, offering us a bench. Ellie made to sit beside me but Mrs Urseau had other ideas.

'There's small beer in a flagon in there, girl,' she ordered, pointing to an open door that led to her kitchen. 'Bring it along for your mistress

– and two tankards with it. Look sharp!'

Ellie stared at me wide-eyed, and for a moment I thought she was going to refuse. I gave her a warning look and she did as she was bidden. I would not usually let such a woman order my friend about so rudely, but I wanted to keep Mrs Urseau in a good temper so that she would answer my questions.

The clockmaker's widow perched opposite me on a stool, and folded her hands stiffly in her lap. Although she was pretty, she had a cold, sharp expression and her lips were thin and tight. She seemed to show more anger than sorrow over the death of her husband. I was not sure how to engage her in conversation. However, it proved easier than I expected.

I leaned forward. 'Your husband's death must have been a terrible shock—'

'That it was!' said the widow sharply. 'And by the hand of Nicholas's own apprentice. One that he thought very well of too. Well, Charles will see justice, and serve him right!' Ellie appeared at this moment with the beer. 'Put it down on the table there,' Mrs Urseau ordered her. 'And pour us good tankards now.'

I was growing annoyed on Ellie's behalf, so

Heaven knows how she kept her own temper in the face of such rudeness. When she had served us our beer, she stood behind Mrs Urseau and pulled such a face at her that I had to bite my lip to keep from bursting out laughing.

'And when you've finished, there's a plate or two wants washing,' added the widow over her shoulder. Ellie stuck out her tongue and stalked off.

'Were you married long?' I asked, composing myself with difficulty.

'Eight long years,' spat Mrs Urseau. 'When I married Nicholas, I thought we would travel with the Court and see all sorts of things. But no. My husband was so wedded to his work we had to stay here. At least *I* did. Even when he went to tend the clocks at Westminster Palace, he did not take me with him.'

A horrible thought occurred to me. Was Mrs Urseau involved in the murder? She was certainly showing no love for her departed husband. I realized that perhaps Mr Urseau dying would benefit her, but my thoughts were interrupted by a loud clattering of pots and pans emanating from the kitchen. Ellie was getting her own back!

Mrs Urseau scowled, and would have got up

had I not spoken again. 'I hope your husband has left you well provided for,' I said.

'You jest, my lady,' said the widow, with a bitter laugh. 'I never saw a penny of his salary – apart from what he gave me for food and drink, that is. You'd think a Royal Clockmaker would buy his wife jewels and fine clothes.'

This made me wonder: if his salary was not going to his wife, then where was it going?

Suddenly a cunning look came over her face. 'Tell me, Lady Grace, have you heard of a box or chest being found in his workshop? A wooden box about the size of a large Bible?'

'I am sorry; I have heard nothing of that,' I said, thinking of the treasure people had been whispering about.

'Then he's hidden it from me!' exclaimed the widow. 'He used to keep it here when we were first married, but after that he took it off somewhere. So now, when I need it . . . Hah! I should have known he wouldn't think of his wife. I was the last on his list. If I'd been one of his new friends, I suppose it would have been a different matter. Them and their meetings!'

I felt a tingle of excitement. These must be the

secret meetings that Charles had mentioned. What was their purpose?

'Where did he meet his friends?' I asked, and then added quickly, 'If we knew who they were, we could discover if they know something of this box.' I did not want Mrs Urseau to start wondering why a Maid of Honour was so interested in a dead clockmaker's secret meetings.

'Everyone thought Nicholas was such a good, kind man, but for the past month he had been so secretive and even more miserly with his money,' she told me – it was clear that she had married him for his money and nothing else. 'His visits to work in other palaces took longer than the tasks warranted. And when I berated him, he would say he had important meetings with his friends, and that one day soon I would be glad of it.'

Money being stashed away, secret meetings . . . When I linked those to his dying words, 'the Queen', a dreadful thought struck me: could Mr Urseau have been plotting against Her Majesty? I reeled at the thought of treason spreading around the Queen's palaces like an evil spider's web, but it would certainly explain why the meetings were so secretive.

'His last meeting was here at Hampton Court,'

Mrs Urseau went on. 'The very night before he was killed.'

'Do you know where?' I asked, hoping she did.

'I guessed straight away,' said the widow with a self-satisfied smile. 'Much as he would like to have kept it from me. His shirt stank of malt on his return. Stupid man not to think I would notice. Me, who had the cleaning of those shirts for eight years! So it had to be at the malting floors. He would have been going again last night if he had lived, and then again tonight.'

There was another dreadful clattering from the other room.

'Mercy!' she exclaimed. 'Methinks you should get rid of that servant, my lady. She's of little use!'

It was certainly time to take our leave, before Ellie did any more damage. I called to her and we left.

We had scarcely gone out of the door when Ellie exploded. '*Girl?* What did she think I was, some sort of skivvy? I'll have her know I'm a tiring woman and not to be ordered about by the likes of her.'

'Your patience did you credit,' I said to pacify her as we hurried back towards the palace. 'Do not give any more thought to Mrs Urseau. We have enough to occupy us without worrying about her.'

Now I knew that the secret meetings had been happening for at least a month, and that one was planned for tonight. And perhaps everyone's high opinion of Mr Urseau was incorrect and he was involved in a treacherous plot against the Queen. I would have to find out.

I must stop. I hear the sweet tones of Mrs Champernowne echoing across the grounds. She is calling for the Maids to attend the Queen. 'Tis well I have more or less finished my entry — except to say that I cannot wait until after supper tonight. I have decided upon a bold course of action. I am somehow going to attend the secret meeting and discover all I can about the treasonous mob who I believe are plotting against our Majestic Sovereign.

The Twenty-seventh Day of September, in the Year of Our Lord 1570

Early morning – a dark hallway

Three of the clock has just struck. I am in a very uncomfortable position, crouched down in the passage outside my bedchamber. The rush lights on the wall are not lit, and so I write by my tiny candle – which I must keep on the floor, lest it be noticed flickering at the window. I cannot write in my chamber for fear of waking the other Maids. Thus I am as cramped as a plum in a preserve. It is most frustrating and therefore fitting, for I have had a most frustrating night.

It started before supper, when Ellie and I had a bit of a quarrel. We had the bedchamber to ourselves, as Lady Sarah and Mary had set off for the other Maids' room so that Sarah could show off the beautiful necklace that had just been gifted to her by Daniel Cheshire. She wanted me to go as well – to have the biggest audience she could – so I had to pretend not to be ready and made a great show of trying to find some earrings.

In truth I wanted to discuss the mystery with Ellie. But I soon wished I had not, for we still cannot agree on Mr Urseau's last words.

'He said "the key",' she insisted. 'Look, I'll show you.' She threw herself upon the floor, eyes closed. 'Just imagine I'm Mr Urseau and I've got a dagger in my chest. I'm mortally wounded but I hear the voice of my apprentice, Charles. I summon my last bit of strength and open my eyes.' She fluttered her eyes dramatically, raising her head a little way off the ground. 'I need to tell Charles about my treasure and I know I've only got a word or two left in me before I die. So I say "the key"' – at this, she waggled her right hand – 'hoping he'll know I mean the key that I'm holding. And then I die.' She flopped her head back on the floor, crossed her eyes and stuck out her tongue.

I clapped my hands. 'What an actor you could be, if women were allowed on the stage,' I laughed. 'But, my dear Ellie, as sure as you are that he said "the key", *I* am certain that his last words were "the Queen" and that there is treason afoot.'

'Why on earth would he say "the Queen"?'

asked Ellie, getting to her feet and fetching my
jewellery box.

'It must have something to do with the secret
meetings,' I said while I sifted through my earrings.
'It is hard to believe that Mr Urseau was a traitor.
He has been at Hampton Court for years and
loyally served not only *our* Queen, but also King
Henry, King Edward and Queen Mary before her.
Why would he suddenly turn to treachery after all
this time?'

'I can't imagine,' agreed Ellie. 'But if he said "the
key" . . .' She took my jewellery box from my
fidgeting hands. 'Now, I think the pearl ones will
do nicely today, my lady.'

She held them out. Each was a gold cross
topped by a single pearl. They were a gift from the
Queen. I thanked Ellie – she is a better judge than
I am of how I look.

'But if he was a conspirator, why did he end up
dead?' I wondered.

'And in a locked room,' Ellie reminded me.

'Aye.' I sighed. 'It always comes back to
that. But there is something I can do to find
out.'

Ellie stopped in the middle of putting my left
earring in. 'Don't tell me,' she said. 'You're going to

sneak in on the meeting tonight, aren't you?' She knew me so well.

'It is the only way to find out what is going on,' I declared, bracing myself for her to forbid me. She surprised me, however.

'Well, if you think you're going alone, then think again,' she said stoutly.

'Thank you, Ellie.' I squeezed her hand, making her wince as the other earring dug into her palm.

'Though whether we'll be welcome is another matter,' she said, rubbing her hand. 'How are you going to explain our presence at their secret meeting when we don't have an invitation?'

I had not thought of that!

'We will say that Mr Urseau told us of the endeavour and we have come in his place,' I said.

'Hope it works,' muttered Ellie. 'Still . . . they can't ask *him*, can they?'

There was a sharp rap at the door, which made us both jump. Ellie opened it and let out a cry. There in the doorway stood a silent cloaked figure, its face hidden by the folds of a big black hood.

'A ghoul!' shrieked Ellie.

'Not with those boots,' I said dryly. 'Hmmm . . . bright red and yellow leather – perfect for an acrobat. Greetings, Masou!'

The wretch pulled back his hood to reveal his grinning face. 'I did not mean to startle you, oh fair ones,' he said. I knew he did! 'But I needed a disguise to come to a Maid of Honour's chamber.'

'Disguise!' snorted Ellie. 'The guards would have run you through without question, looking like that!'

She pulled him into the room and shut the door.

'You have come at an opportune moment,' I said, and told him of our planned escapade. 'Will you come with us? We could use your protection.'

'I am at your service,' he said, making as if to bow to the floor; but his foot got caught in the heavy black cloak and he toppled forward. Of course, being Masou, he quickly turned it into a forward roll over my bed and was soon on his feet again, cloak flying out behind. 'Where will we be going?' he asked, as if nothing untoward had occurred.

'Mrs Urseau believes that the meetings take place at the malting floors,' I told him.

'They are by the rabbit warrens in the Home Park,' said Masou. 'Near enough to the brewery for ease of transport but far enough away so that the Queen is not aware of the stench.'

'When do you think the meeting might take place?' asked Ellie.

'After nightfall,' I said, 'when all is quiet at Court. Which will make it easier for us to leave here – but what of the guards on the gate?'

'I will find a way out through the gardens,' said Masou. 'Nothing is too hard for the Queen's favourite acrobat.'

'I'm surprised that hood fits over your big head!' grunted Ellie, pulling at his cloak.

I smiled. 'And while we are on the subject of your disguise, why have you come to my chamber?'

'You asked me to keep my eyes and ears open, and of course,' he said, 'I have performed that task to perfection. I have found out something that will be of interest to you.'

'Tell me then.' I was impatient to hear.

Masou settled himself on my bed and made a great show of arranging his cloak before continuing. Maddening!

'It concerns one of the palace porters,' he said. 'He was telling all who would listen about his duties for Mr Urseau on the very day of the murder.'

'Was it Jem Ainsworth?' I asked.

'Yes.' Masou was surprised. 'How did you know that?'

'You're not the only one keeping your eyes and ears open,' scoffed Ellie.

'Then you will not need me to tell you where he is now,' said Masou, getting up and making for the door.

'Don't you dare leave until you have!' Ellie grabbed his cloak and held it fast.

'Do not torture me, cruel girl,' croaked Masou, pretending to choke. 'Mr Ainsworth is in the Privy Kitchen.'

Ellie and I almost knocked him over in our haste to get through the door. This porter was the third item on my list of things to investigate, and I had already learned at least something of the meetings and the treasure box.

When we arrived at the Privy Kitchen, Jem Ainsworth was once again sitting in state by the fire. We were just making our way over to him when Mr Hatton suddenly appeared in the archway. God's Oath! I thought. Was I never going to be able to speak with Jem! Mr Hatton's face showed a mixture of surprise and irritation. I could hazard a guess about what he was thinking – *What is that meddling Maid doing here?*

I had to speak quickly. 'Good evening, Mr

Hatton,' I said sweetly. 'I am on an errand for my Lady Sarah.'

He raised an eyebrow at me and I felt compelled to say more. 'I need some sour milk—' Curses! That was a foolish thing to say. I would be in the dairy if I needed milk, not the kitchen. '*Boiled* milk, that is,' I gabbled on. 'And . . .' I cast my eyes over the nearest table, desperately trying to find some other ingredient. A kitchen maid was cutting up vegetables. 'And spinach. It's for a face cream, I believe.'

Now I knew I was on safe ground, for Mr Hatton is a man and of course knows nothing about ladies' potions, real or otherwise. I could see his eyes glazing over as I spoke. Then he nodded curtly to me and turned to Jem Ainsworth. The fat old porter had jumped to his feet on Mr Hatton's entrance.

'Come with me to my private lodgings, man,' said Mr Hatton. 'And have your cart ready. I need you to move a portrait for me.'

He strode out, with Jem trotting at his heels, looking as proud as a peacock to have been chosen by the Captain of the Queen's Guard.

Mr Hatton may be pompous with me at times, but he is a good man and a loyal servant to the

Queen, so I felt a little guilty at having lied to him. However, I got my comeuppance, for in the next instant a beaming kitchen servant came up to me with a jug of steaming sour milk. It smelled revolting and looked even worse, for it had green bits floating in it. There was only one possible course of action: I thanked her and carried it out. Ellie began to guffaw like an ass, but soon ceased when I gave her the jug to carry.

'We will take it to my bedchamber,' I said, for I could think of nothing else to do with it. 'Mayhap Lady Sarah will have a use for it after all.' Why had I not thought of asking for something nicer? A bowl of blackberries, for example.

Back in our chamber, Ellie held her nose dramatically and dumped the jug down in the corner. Then she turned to me.

'Listen, Grace,' she said. 'I've been thinking. This plan to go to the secret meeting tonight – it's awful perilous. Won't you change your mind?'

'No, Ellie,' I told her. 'If there is a plot to kill our gracious Sovereign and my beloved godmother, then I will do everything in my power to prevent it . . . and expose it.'

I had been wondering whether I should have warned the Queen. The thought of Her Majesty dying by an assassin's hand suddenly made cold fingers run up my spine. It would not be the first time such an attempt had been made, as I knew to my cost. My dear mother had died drinking poisoned wine intended for Her Majesty.

But I reminded myself that I had no proof. Besides, the Queen had already threatened me with Latin translations for seeing mysteries where she believed there to be none. And I had yet to uncover a more likely suspect than Charles Doute. I resolved to hold until I had something to put before the Queen. And I would not lightly charge anyone with treason. Traitors are tortured and put to death.

As it went on, the day did not improve. Supper is best forgotten for I embarrassed myself greatly. I was sitting near the Queen, right between Lucy Throckmorton and Carmina, who were having a lively conversation across me. I think it was about silver aiglets. It seemed everyone else was still talking about the murder. There was no doubt in anyone's mind that it was Charles Doute who had plunged the dagger into Mr Urseau's chest.

'The matter has been referred to the Board of Green Cloth, of course, because the foul deed was done here at Court, and therefore close to Her

Majesty,' said Sir Pelham, reaching for a pork pasty. 'Mr Hatton is to report to them. But there is nothing to report. The murderer is locked up and they will soon have finished with the dreadful business.'

This meant that little investigation was being done. Yet I was still not convinced that Charles Doute had killed his master.

At that moment I caught a glimpse of something out of the corner of my eye. Someone was approaching the Queen and I saw a flash of silver in the candlelight.

My heart thudded – I knew it was an assassin come to strike her down in front of us all! I leaped to my feet and dived at the man, but he turned out to be a servant carrying a shiny platter of herrings. Servant, Maid and herrings all went tumbling across the room, crashing in a heap against the tapestried wall. I struggled to sit up. Everyone was gawping at me.

''Zounds!' I heard Sir Pelham gasp. 'The Maid has lost her wits!'

Mr Hatton and Daniel Cheshire were soon at my side, helping me to my feet.

'I am sorry,' I twittered. 'I stood up to find my tiring woman and caught my foot in my skirts.'

'And there was I thinking you had taken a dislike to the fish!' came the Queen's merry voice. I was very grateful to Her Majesty, for everyone laughed and turned to her. I apologized to the poor serving man and made note to send Ellie to him with a few coins in recompense. Still, if it *had* been an assassin . . .

I was greatly relieved when supper was over and all memories of my odd behaviour were driven away by the superb performance of Mr Somers's troupe. Tonight they enacted the Harvest made glorious by the Sun, Elizabeth. The Queen beamed upon the tumblers as if she truly were the sun. Gypsy Pete was very sweet. He portrayed a seed that grew into a strong ear of wheat. Then French Louis mimed cutting him down with his scythe and threw him over his shoulder. Everyone clapped tremendously as the wheat waved and grinned before being carried off.

After all the excitement, the Queen dismissed us and we made for our beds. I was hoping that my fellow Maids would be abed and snoring well before I had to sneak out. I was all ready to put some pillows under my bedclothes. It is a strange thing to boast about, but I am becoming quite skilled at making it look as if someone is asleep in my place. If only I could get the pillow to breathe or, better still, talk in its sleep!

Anyhow, although Mary was deeply asleep, Lady Sarah was wide awake. She kept sitting up in bed and prattling on about how wonderful Mr Cheshire is. I am truly happy she has such a devoted admirer, but a love-struck Sarah was hard to deal with, especially when I wanted to be off and out.

'He has written me two sonnets and an ode, Grace,' she sighed, clutching some papers to her heart. 'How can I sleep with such words calling to be read over and over again?'

There was a candlestick near her bed. Was it possible to hit her over the head with it in a way that would put her to sleep but not cause any lasting damage? Probably not. I would really like to have thrown a shoe at her the way Her Majesty does when she is in a temper with her Maids. No, I would have to use gentler means to get her snoring. I once bored her to sleep with conversation, but she had been given a lot of laudanum at the time so I could not take all the credit!

Then I had a brilliant idea. 'Lady Anne was telling me the other day how dangerous lack of sleep is to the complexion,' I said idly. Sarah fixed me with a horrified stare. 'Oh yes,' I carried on, 'she heard it was sure to bring spots popping up by the score.'

Sarah carefully folded up the papers and placed them under her pillow. 'I would be grateful if you would stop your chatter, Grace,' she said, throwing herself down and pulling her blanket up over her shoulders. 'And blow out that candle. Some of us would like to get some beauty sleep.'

I wanted to retort that I was not as prone to chitchat as some, but bit my tongue and raised my eyes to the Heavens instead. Within minutes, Sarah had joined Mary in a snoring contest and I could fill my bed with pillows.

I tiptoed out into the passage to find Ellie waiting for me. She led me down the back stairs to the kitchens, where we were not so likely to meet any guards.

We crept through the Master Carpenter's Court and found Masou. He led us across Pond Yard. The way was well lit with torches so we had to keep to the shadows whenever possible.

'Down!' hissed Masou suddenly. We dived behind a hedge – and just in time, for two of the Gentlemen Guard were walking by. When they had moved on, we made for the wall. Old King Henry had built this wall to separate his palace from his deer park. He must have thought it a good idea, but I was wishing he had not built it so high.

Luckily Ellie and Masou were there to heave and push, and I made it over to the other side. Using the wall as a guide in the dim moonlight, we hurried along to the barns that housed the malting floors. The nearest one was in darkness. We could smell the malt long before we reached it.

'That one will have the barley spread all over it,' Masou told us. 'They will rake it several times until it has turned into sweet, sticky malt. The men of mystery must be using the next barn.'

'How do you know all this?' asked Ellie, trying not to sound too impressed.

Masou tapped his nose. 'I have my ways,' was all my annoying friend would say.

As we turned the corner, the other shed came into sight. We could see flickering candlelight and shadows within.

'Stay here out of sight, Masou,' I whispered. 'We will scream if we need you.'

'I will be alert,' he promised, and he sank down into the darkness of a bush.

'You'd better be,' grunted Ellie. Her eyes were

wide with fright but she stayed by my side as I crept towards the door of the shed. I had no idea if the plotters would believe my story that Mr Urseau had invited me to join them, but I had to find out exactly what these secret meetings were about. The Queen's life depended upon it, I was certain. Just as I was certain that the clockmaker's last words had indeed been 'the Queen'.

'What are we going to say, Grace?' whimpered Ellie. 'You're the Queen's god-daughter. Why would you be here plotting against her?'

'I must make them believe that I am displeased with her for some reason,' I said quietly. 'Let us hope that they will welcome someone so close to their intended victim.'

We reached the door. I was about to push it open a little when a voice behind us demanded, 'Who goes there?'

Some minutes later

Hell's teeth! My stub of a candle suddenly flickered just now and went out. I had to go back to my bedchamber and scrabble about in the darkness to

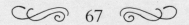

find a new one – and a tinder to light it. The noise of that was enough to wake the dead in this silent palace! However, no one has stirred, God be praised, so I will continue – although this new candle gleams like the sun. I hope no one notices its light.

I felt Ellie's hand grasping my sleeve as a tall figure stepped out of the shadows. I had forgotten that of course there would be someone guarding the door. What would happen if they did not believe my claim that I wished to join them? My heart was beating so hard in my chest that I almost forgot the part I was to play. Then I saw who stood before us. It was Stephen Morling, one of the Gentleman of Her Majesty's Guard. I was shocked that such a trusted man could betray his Queen. I swallowed hard and began.

'Mr Morling, I am most glad to see you,' I said, trying to sound as conspiratorial as possible. 'I hope I have come to the right place. I am a friend of poor Mr Urseau. He told me of your . . . meetings.' Stephen Morling gave a start of surprise. 'Do not fear I will give you away,' I went on quickly. 'I have the same . . . interests as that noble man. It was his dearest wish that we work together to achieve our aims.'

'His dearest wish,' echoed Ellie in solemn agreement. Mr Morling gave her a suspicious stare and her grip tightened on my sleeve.

'My tiring woman is privy to our business,' I told him. 'You can trust her absolutely. Now, sir,' I added, sounding bolder than I felt, 'I am impatient to attend the meeting. Pray, lead me to it.'

I must say I expected to be questioned closely about my motives and was fully ready with my complaints of cruel treatment from Her Majesty – all invented of course. Weren't these men deterred by the thought of the torture and executions that surely awaited them when they were caught?

But Mr Morling simply bowed. 'In truth, I am not surprised to see you here, my lady,' he said.

I felt a surge of anger against this man who could so willingly believe that I would ever betray My Liege. I had to bite my tongue – and prepared myself to say terrible things about the Queen when I came face to face with her enemies.

I tried to keep my breathing slow and steady. But I was not as calm as I appeared. I began to be troubled that Stephen Morling had accepted my story without question. Why would he do that? Unless, my fevered imagination told me, we were walking into a trap! It was too late for me to turn back now. I needed to know all about the conspirators, and this was the only way to find out.

Mr Morling rapped a short rhythm on the door – no doubt the agreed password among the treacherous clan. At first there was silence, then we heard slow footsteps from within. A clanking latch was lifted and a chink of light appeared as the door creaked open. We were led into a large barn-like room. I followed the Guard, taking bold steps, which became more of a limp as Ellie was hanging onto my arm.

'All will be well,' I whispered to her, though I wasn't sure I believed it myself.

The first thing that hit me was the acrid smell of old barley, which made my eyes water. No matter, I thought. It might add to my pretence of passion against the Queen. The second thing was the group of about twenty cloaked men standing together at the far end of the long, empty room. Their faces were lit by flickering candlelight and they looked utterly shocked at the sight of a Maid of Honour and her tiring woman in their midst. As we approached the silent group, my heart pounded. I recognized the faces of one or two more Gentlemen Guards and some of Her Majesty's own courtiers! They were not those close to the Queen, but none of them would I have thought of as possible traitors. I began to berate myself for not having seen signs of unrest at Court. I had truly failed in my position as Her Majesty's Lady Pursuivant, to have had absolutely no idea of such a large group of villains conspiring in our midst.

There was another shock to come – one that nearly made me catch my breath and give myself away. In the middle of the group stood Monsieur Danton. I kept my face expressionless, but I could feel my jaw clenching with anger – the Queen's own dancing master had betrayed the trust she so graciously put in him. As soon as he saw it was me, Monsieur Danton's eyes widened and he stepped back, covering his mouth and nose with his handkerchief. He clearly did not want me to recognize him. Faith! I thought. The prisons will be full to bursting when this villainous band are found out. And I was determined that they would be.

Mr Morling stood before the group. 'We are all gathered,' he said. I was surprised that such a quiet, mild-mannered man should be the chosen leader, and that he had left no one on guard outside the door. What arrogance!

'But why is Lady Grace Cavendish here?' demanded a voice.

'Peace, Geoffrey,' Stephen Morling replied. 'Mr Urseau told her of our purpose and she has come at his invitation. She is privy to our secret mission and wishes to work with us to achieve our end.'

At the name of the dead clockmaker there were low mutterings and head-shakings around the group. I glanced at Ellie, and saw that her eyes were flashing with fear. I guessed she was thinking the same as I was: were the conspirators aggrieved with Mr Urseau? Could it be that he was not only a traitor to the Queen, but had then double-crossed his fellow plotters? Perhaps it was *they* who had had him killed! So if it now appeared that we were friendly with Mr Urseau, we must surely be in danger ourselves. Were we about to suffer the same fate as Her Majesty's clockmaker?

'Let us keep silence for a moment before we begin,' Mr Morling went on, 'for our dead brother who put all these events into motion. Think on Nicholas's memory.'

The other men bowed their heads, and we quickly did the same. Ellie slipped her hand into mine for reassurance and I gave it a squeeze. I was relieved to find that I had been wrong. Mr Urseau could not have betrayed the plotters or they would not have spoken so fondly of him. For the time being, we were safe and I found myself actually *grateful* that Mr Urseau was indeed a traitor!

But then another thought occurred to me: if we were caught here, among these men, what would Her Majesty think? Surely she would believe that I was not here to join with their plans. My palms began to sweat as my mind was filled with images of Hatton and the Gentlemen of the Guard marching towards the barns to capture the plotters. Would Ellie and I be arrested for treason and tortured until we confessed? And what would the Gentlemen Guards do to Masou, who was on watch outside?

'We must to our task.' I had been quite wrapped up in my worried thoughts and the voice of Mr Morling made me start. 'We all know that what we are undertaking is difficult. But we must not give up. We must see it through . . . to the end.'

'Aye!' said the courtier called Geoffrey. 'There are no cowards here.'

'Though I confess I cannot sleep nights after our meetings,' said an older man. 'I do toss and turn and I think my wife would kick me out of bed if she could.'

'I hope you have not breathed a word of what we are about,' said Mr Morling sharply.

'Not I!' he replied. 'I am true to the cause. Besides, she will find out soon enough.'

'So will the Queen!' declared Geoffrey. At that everyone laughed loudly and nudged his neighbour. I felt Ellie's nails dig into my hand. I turned to her and forced a smile onto my face, although in my heart I felt nothing but fury towards these terrible men. Yet we had to join in or we would be discovered. Ellie let out what I can only describe as a hysterical cackle and did not stop until everyone else had gone quiet.

'Let us begin,' declared Stephen, and the men quickly formed two lines facing each other, leaving us standing alone, quite forgotten. I felt a thrill of horror. Were they preparing to commit their nefarious crime right at this moment? And what would our part be?

Monsieur Danton stood at the end of the lines. ''Ave your instruments at the ready!'

'Oh no! They're going to do it now!' hissed Ellie, looking around wildly for a means of escape. 'They mean to march off and attack the Queen as she sleeps! For the love of God, Grace, let's get away from here and warn someone.'

Several men at the far end of the lines reached into their cloaks. I prepared myself to see daggers and other instruments of death . . . But, not in my wildest imaginings could I have pictured the scene that unfolded in front of us. I was convinced I must be dreaming: the men at the far end of the lines had not pulled out daggers, but lutes and sackbuts! In a moment they had struck up a merry tune and the two lines of gentlemen had begun to *dance* – very badly – with what I assumed were imaginary partners! Ellie and I watched in stunned amazement.

'*Non, non, non!*' exclaimed Monsieur Danton as two of the hapless dancers collided in the middle. 'You are so clumsy . . . so *English* in your dancing. Be light on your feet!' The dancing master skipped into the middle of the group to demonstrate. '*Hélas!* You will never be ready to show this to the Queen at the Michaelmas Feast.'

Suddenly it all made sense. These men were no conspirators – far from it. They did not wish to kill their monarch – they simply wanted to please her by learning how to dance properly. There was a sort of snorting sound in my ear and I turned to see Ellie convulsed and holding her sides. I tried to keep a solemn face – after all, these men were doing their best, even though most of them looked like nervous chickens – but the sight of them and the relief that we were safe from imminent death got the better of me.

'*Mesdemoiselles!*' exclaimed Monsieur Danton as we giggled helplessly. (My goodness, that man is most light of foot: I had not heard him approach!) 'Do not laugh at our efforts – especially you, Lady Grace, for I think you 'ave come to join us, *non*?'

I noticed that the dancing master stood at a careful distance from me, handkerchief in hand.

'I am sorry, Monsewer Danton,' gasped Ellie, wiping her eyes with her sleeve. 'It's just that we thought that you . . . that you were all— *Ow!*'

'Of course I wish to join in,' I said with a gracious smile as I elbowed Ellie in the ribs to silence her. I was not about to let her tell the truth about why we had come to the secret meeting. 'I am eager to begin.' With that I moved towards him.

Monsieur Danton promptly took a step back and waved the handkerchief. 'But your sneefle? Your cold?' he said in a panic. 'Do not come near!'

So that was why he had covered his face earlier. He had remembered my earlier 'cold' and seen me as the bringer of sickness!

'I was mistaken,' I reassured him. 'Some flowers brought to one of the Maids must have made my nose itch. It was nothing more than that.'

Monsieur Danton beamed and held out an elegant hand to me. 'Then you will be most useful to me and my pupils – if you are careful with your feet,' he added knowingly.

I could have kicked myself for not thinking more quickly. If I had claimed I was still suffering, the fussy monsieur would have dismissed me straight away for fear of catching my illness and we could have escaped.

Soon I found myself standing in the middle of the dancers. I had to partner the dancing master as he showed the correct gentleman's steps in the Pavane, or how to do a cutting step. I wished Ellie could have taken my place under everyone's scrutiny. Even though she only knows the steps I have taught her in the privacy of my bedchamber, I was certain she would make a better job of this than I.

At last Monsieur Danton let me go – but the torture was not over. I was immediately approached by a line of courtiers begging me to be their practice partner. There was no peace for the wicked – and I had been wicked in my imaginings about these innocent men.

Then I thought of a way to bring a smile to Ellie's face. 'Gentlemen, I fear I cannot share myself between you. Some of you must wait your turn. But do not forget that there is another lady here who would be glad to partner one of you.'

There was a rush for Ellie, and soon I saw her stepping nimbly across the room.

'Thanks, Grace,' she called as we passed in the Galliard. 'I never thought the night would turn out so good!'

She was having a wonderful time, but I was wondering when this madness would end. Would I be forced to dance all night – and get no further with my investigations? And I was leaving a trail of crushed toes behind me too!

My partner for the Volta was Mr Morling. In between listening to sharp instructions and French expletives from the dancing master, I managed to ask him how the classes had first started. 'For as soon as Mr Urseau talked of them to me, I was in such a flurry to join you that I scarcely listened to the rest of what he said,' I exclaimed, with a silly giggle.

'Don't you remember,' Mr Morling began, 'that terrible night a month since at Whitehall Palace?'

I confessed that I could not think what he meant.

He went on as we stepped around the room. 'Poor Geoffrey committed the dreadful sin of catching the lace on the Queen's new skirt with his foot in the middle of a Sarabande. As the material ripped, Her Majesty gave a shriek the like of which I have never heard before – and never wish to again. It stopped us in our tracks. Poor Geoffrey could do nothing but grovel on his knees until the Queen had finished shouting at him.'

Mr Morling kicked left instead of right and hit my shin. I quickly turned my wince into a smile.

'Of course, he deserved it, you understand,' he said after he had apologized. 'Then Her Majesty turned to the rest of us! She informed the room that there was scarcely a handful of good dancers at Court and therefore only a handful who could call themselves true men. Surely you remember it, Lady Grace?'

I did recall the incident, once he'd reminded me. The Queen had been in a foul mood that day and I had felt sorry for the man who had borne the brunt of her fiery temper.

'The Queen is the finest judge of the dance there could be,' Stephen Morling continued with a mournful look, 'and I was wounded by her words. Others felt the same, including our dear Mr Urseau. And so our secret meetings began – we have them at whatever palace we visit.'

At this he lifted me high in the air! I had been so intent on his words that I had forgotten this was to come in the Volta and whacked him in the face with my arm by mistake!

'I must confess I was surprised to find that Mr Urseau was one of your number,' I said, a little breathlessly, when my feet were on the ground again.

Stephen Morling rubbed his chin. 'Mr Urseau was the founder of the group and persuaded Monsieur Danton to teach us privately. They were friends. It seems that Nicholas had nursed an ambition to learn to dance better ever since he married his wife, for she is young, fair and quite demanding.'

I regretted I had thought the clockmaker a traitor, and rather pitied him for having to go to such lengths for such a shrewish wife.

Mr Morling grasped me round the waist again but I was ready for the lift this time and did him no injury.

'We are almost ready to demonstrate our

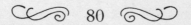

improvement to Her Majesty,' he panted. 'At the Michaelmas celebrations we will amaze the Court.'

At last the dancing came to an end, and to add insult to injury, I had to line up and pay Monsieur Danton for my lesson – and for Ellie's! The dancing master beamed at me as I dropped the coins into his full purse.

'Ah, Lady Grace, you have improved so much tonight! But I do not like the thought of a Maid of Honour joining our classes when we are only gentlemen 'ere. 'Owever, I shall breathe not a word to good Mrs Champernowne.'

I volunteered to never come again, but I was having no luck.

'*Alors!*' Monsieur Danton's face lit up. 'I 'ave an idea. I will give you your own private lesson each day – after you have practised with the other Maids, of course.'

'Of course,' I said, curtsying. I had to hide the horror on my face. I grasped Ellie firmly by the hand and made sure we were first out of the door.

We found Masou asleep under a hedge.

'Some bodyguard you are!' hissed Ellie. 'We could have been killed, brought back to life and then killed again, and you wouldn't have known a thing about it.'

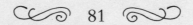

'You think I would let you go in there and not keep an eye on you?' said Masou, rubbing his eyes. 'As soon as you had gone I peered in through the window. You went to seek out cunning plotters but all you found were prancing plodders! What was that all about?'

Ellie told him the whole story.

'Well, Grace,' Masou said gravely, 'you thought you would be in danger, but it was your poor partners who suffered, from what I could see.'

'Let me show you some of the new steps I have learned,' I said. 'This one is called the Toe Squasher!'

But Masou jumped nimbly out of my way.

I am no nearer to discovering why Mr Urseau was killed, but at least he was not a traitor. I can dismiss one of the three items on my list: the secret meetings had nothing to do with Mr Urseau's murder. It is down to the treasure and the porter. And now to bed, for the first rays of dawn are creeping through the window.

It has just struck me what Stephen Morling meant when he said he was not surprised to see me at the secret meeting. He had not thought me a conspirator, but a poor dancer. It may be true, but it is not pleasant to hear it from someone who has three left feet if I have two! However, it is better than being thought a traitor, I suppose.

And now truly to bed!

Eleven of the clock in the evening
Back in my bedchamber

I am in my bed again, candle on a shelf by my elbow and daybooke on my lap. The Court has retired early to bed. I have much to write, for it has been an intriguing day. And when I have written my fill, I will sleep until morning – despite this strange odour that wafts under my nose every few minutes. I wonder if there is some trouble with the sewers here at Hampton Court Palace. Still, I am looking forward to a blissful sleep after practically none last night!

I woke at seven this morning but was ushered back to bed by Mrs Champernowne, who thought I was ill, for I looked so pale. And to my 'sorrow', this meant I missed the Maids' dancing lesson. (I must be careful and miss Monsieur Danton's private lesson as well.)

When I next woke, it was early afternoon. Faith, if this carries on I shall become an owl and wake only at night!

As I made my way to the Queen's Watching Chamber, I tried to sort out my thoughts. I had to find a way to speak to the porter, and I also needed to find out more about the box his wife was after and whether it was the rumoured treasure. And as I thought on it, I had to admit that perhaps Ellie was right about the clockmaker's last words. If Mr Urseau was referring to the key in his hand, then perhaps that was the key to his treasure.

The Maids and Ladies sat on cushions, embroidering. I like the Watching Chamber. The windows are built in alcoves, which makes the chamber very light. The walls are covered in tapestries and have afforded me many a distraction from a boring speech or poetry reading – especially the tapestry depicting the Death of Hercules.

Her Majesty was having a quiet conference with Mr Secretary Cecil. Other ministers hovered nearby, hoping to speak with her. Weighty matters of State, no doubt. It might have been two days since Mr Urseau's murder and the supposed culprit being locked up, but talk of the event had not abated in the least. Lady Anne Courtenay was telling all around her that, in her opinion, Charles Doute had shifty eyes and that proved him a murderer. (She was still croaky despite Mrs Champernowne's posset.)

Suddenly the Queen looked in our direction. 'Are you still talking of the death of my clockmaker?' she demanded. We all jumped to our feet, needles and threads scattering across the wooden floor. 'I wonder at your interest in this ghastly business. You would do better to find new topics to occupy your time.'

She waved at us to sit again and turned back to Mr Cecil. In obedience to the Queen, Carmina began to tell a comic tale of a man up at Hampton Wick who had been so drunk he had mistaken the green water of the Wick pond for a meadow and tried to walk upon the surface. Her – really rather humorous – story concluded, we were quickly back to the murder, but in hushed tones this time. Talk of the murder was incessant. Indeed, the only lulls in conversation came when the Queen beckoned over the next in line. We would all stay obediently quiet while the petitioner introduced himself, only taking up our topic again when he and Her Majesty were deep in conversation.

As I listened to the condemnation of Charles by all around me, I felt I could not join in. A guilty man would not have lingered at the scene of his crime. It did not make any sense for him to do that. True enough, Ellie and I had come upon him mere moments after we heard Mr Urseau's cry, but Charles could have concocted a much better story than simply saying he was fumbling with his keys. And he had time to think of a good excuse, for Ellie and I did not immediately accuse him of anything. It was not until the carpenter turned up that Charles had to give any account of his appearance at the side of his dying master. He had seemed so genuine in his grief as well.

I thought more about that little key in Mr Urseau's hand. I could not quite recall its shape and I had no hope of looking at it now that it lay in Mr Hatton's pouch. But I could visit the workshop and look at keyholes. That might give me some sort of clue. I wanted to go at once, but the queue of ministers and petitioners for the Queen's time was long and slow moving. We would be expected to sit here until they were done. I looked in the direction of the Queen and was struck with an idea that might speed my departure from the

Watching Chamber, though it was really rather risky.

No matter, I told myself. If I was right about Charles Doute, an innocent man was languishing in a cell and this would not do. I took action.

Lady Jane was whispering into Lucy's ear. From the scared and excited look on Lucy's face, I knew they had to be discussing the murder.

'What is this?' I hissed across Lucy. 'Tell me.'

'Well' – Lady Jane spoke in a hushed tone – 'I heard that Charles Doute is heavily in debt because he gambles – or was it that he is a drunkard? No matter, it gives him the clearest motive for killing his master to get to the treasure.'

'What was that?' I hissed again, cupping my hand to my ear. In truth, I had heard it all perfectly clearly but, for my purpose, I had to pretend that my ears had failed me.

Lady Jane repeated it a little louder than before.

'I cannot hear you,' I said apologetically.

A look of impatience came over Jane's face. She had not noticed that the Queen was about to welcome the next gentlemen in line and that everyone else had therefore fallen silent.

'I SAID, CHARLES GAMBLES AND

DRINKS SO THAT IS WHY HE NEEDED
THE TREASURE!'

The whole chamber gasped as Jane almost yelled
these words at me. Those of us who dared to look
at the Queen saw a stare like ice in January.

'I would that the Maids and Ladies leave the
chamber immediately,' she said severely. 'For my
own comfort, you understand. I do not wish to
have cold feet but that is what I will suffer after I
have thrown my slippers at you!'

We bowed and curtsied, bundling ourselves
backwards out of the door before she got the chance
to carry out this threat. We hastened along the
gallery, all giggling – well, all except for Lady Jane.

'You did that on purpose, Grace!' she
complained. 'And the Queen will believe it was all
my fault. How could you?'

'I did not mean to get you into trouble,' I said.
'But look at the result. We have the afternoon to
ourselves and it is a fine autumn day. Let us be
outside, for that is where most of the gentlemen
will be.'

I was hoping to lose my companions and carry
on with my investigations!

'You will not get round me that easily,' Jane said
stuffily as we went down to the Clock Court. 'I am

most annoyed and—' She broke off as she suddenly spotted Sir Thomas loitering nearby. She shot me one last dirty look, took hold of Carmina's arm and resolutely turned the other way. 'Ah, look, Carmina. There are Sir Mark and Mr Swinburne. Where are they making off to?'

'Archery practice,' said Carmina as the two handsome courtiers passed by with bows and arrows.

'Then what are we waiting here for?' demanded Jane, pulling Carmina after her. 'We shall watch.' Lucy and Mary followed, and Sarah went in search of 'a quiet corner to sit and think'. Hah! A quiet corner where she hoped Mr Cheshire would find her, more likely.

I stood for a moment looking up at the beautiful astronomical clock that Mr Urseau built for the old King Henry thirty years ago. I imagine the face is near five yards across – it truly is a thing of wonder. The clock tells the hour and the number of days since the beginning of the year. It even tells the time of the high tide at London Bridge.

'I vow to you by your clock, Mr Urseau,' I said to myself, 'that I will find your murderer and bring him to justice.'

There, I had made a promise. I *had* to solve the mystery now!

I decided to go in search of Ellie. It took me some time, as I saw Monsieur Danton tripping towards me from the Base Court and had to scurry round by the Privy Kitchen to avoid him. But what luck! Ellie was there asking for some lemon juice to attack a grease stain on one of my wrist ruffs.

'Come with me, Ellie,' I called. 'I have something for you to do.'

'Yes, my lady,' she said obediently – and loudly enough for all the kitchen servants to hear. Oh, if only they knew how she treats me in private!

'I wasn't really going to clean your ruffs,' she whispered. 'I was looking to see if Jem was there, but he must be actually doing some work for a change. There was not a sign of him.'

'No matter,' I said. 'I have been pondering over Mr Urseau's last words. Mayhap you were right and he did say "the key".'

Ellie beamed at me. 'He did; I'm sure of it.' She could not resist a little gloat. 'I knew you'd come round to my way of thinking.'

'Then we must discover which key,' I said, ignoring this last comment.

'The one in his hand, of course,' declared Ellie.

'Probably.' I was thinking hard. 'A key that small would most likely be used to wind a clock, or open a small box like the one Mrs Urseau described. We need to go to the workshop.'

We made our way there. We could hear the distant sounds of sawing and hammering from the carpenters' room, but there was no one about in the passageways. I grasped the handle of the door – it was locked!

'What a goose I am!' I said to Ellie. 'Mr Hatton will have locked it, of course.'

We stood there for some minutes, racking our brains. Then Ellie gave a little clap of her hands.

'Masou!' she cried. 'He has the skill necessary to pick a lock. He's done it before – remember, when there was the mystery of the man beneath the ice at the Frost Fair, and we were locked in that closet and fearing for our very lives? He got us out right enough that day.'

'Then we must find Masou,' I declared, and we set off in search.

The troupe were practising in the Fountain Court. It was easy to spot Masou, for he was balanced at the top of a human pyramid. Ellie and I hid in a doorway. Then I leaned out and waved to him until he saw me. I beckoned to him to come. He shook his head and pointed down at the acrobats supporting him. This caused him to lose balance slightly and sent a shiver right through the tower.

'Stay still!' complained Paul. He and his twin brother, Percival, formed the second tier – it was their shoulders that Masou was standing on. 'You'll have us all over.'

The pyramid righted itself. I beckoned again, urgently this time. Masou threw his hands in the air in exasperation and this time the acrobats wobbled violently. It was very comical to see Masou swaying this way and that, flailing his arms like a windmill to keep his balance. Ellie and I creased up with laughter. Despite all his efforts, Masou fell, twisted in the air, and of course landed nimbly on his feet. His fellow tumblers were not so lucky. The pyramid collapsed on the ground in a great mess of arms and legs!

Mr Somers appeared. 'What's going on here?' he asked.

'It was Masou,' said Paul, untangling himself from French Louis. 'He fidgeted as if he had ants in his hose.'

Percival grunted in agreement. 'Calls himself

the best acrobat in the troupe as well!'

'He made the tumblers tumble, eh?' Mr Somers's face was stern but his words were mild enough.

'I am sorry,' said Masou. 'I was—'

'Get you away and fetch everyone some small beer to make amends,' said Mr Somers. 'You can run off your fidgets and mind you do not return until you have.'

Masou grinned and scampered over to our hiding place. 'What is it you want, ladies,' he said, 'that you should cause the collapse of our human tower and put the dwarf twins in a temper?'

'I need you to pick the lock of the clockmaker's workroom,' I told him.

Masou's eyes widened in mock horror and he threw a hand dramatically over his heart. 'You would have me perform a burglary?' he said. 'I, the Queen's favourite fool, being asked to do something illegal! What are you thinking of?'

'Shut your trap, Masou,' said Ellie, pinching him on the arm, 'and get along with us.'

'I will join you there in an instant,' he said with a bow. 'Let me first fetch my tools. But I must be quick, else I will be missed.'

We were soon back at the door to the

workshop. Masou bent to the keyhole and began fiddling with a thin piece of metal.

'Hmmm,' he said. 'I do not believe this will prove difficult. I just need to—'

He stopped. We had all heard a dreaded voice echoing round the corner. It was Mrs Fadget, the deputy laundress, and she was berating one of the carpenters for something.

'She is coming this way,' I gasped. 'Quick, Ellie – stop her.'

Ellie gulped. Mrs Fadget had made her life a misery when she was a lowly laundrymaid and I know that she has avoided her as much as possible ever since.

However, brave Ellie squared her shoulders and set off towards the whining voice. Masou and I heard the whole of their exchange.

'Good morrow, Mrs Fadget.' Ellie sounded polite enough.

'What are you doing here, Ellie Bunting?' came the harsh reply. 'You've no business being in these parts.'

Mrs Fadget bears a grudge that Ellie escaped from her authority at the laundry. I tensed. How would Ellie respond?

'I'm on an errand for my mistress, Lady Grace,' I

heard her say boldly. 'And it is urgent. Something for the Queen herself.'

'Yes, well.' Mrs Fadget seemed lost for words. Clever Ellie to bring Her Majesty into it. The miserable laundress would never dare countermand any order of the Queen's. 'Then I won't keep you.'

We heard footsteps coming our way. It sounded as if Mrs Fadget was about to come round the corner, where she would see Masou and me for sure.

'Mrs Fadget!' Ellie almost shouted. 'You don't want to go that way.'

'And why not, pray?'

'I just came from there,' Ellie told her. 'And I wouldn't go back that way, not for all the treasure in Spain.'

'What are you babbling about, girl?' came Mrs Fadget's sneering voice.

'I heard something as I passed poor Mr Urseau's room,' said Ellie. 'The most horrible cry and rattling of chains. I believe it was the clockmaker himself come back from the grave in search of his murderer. But that's not all. His blood-stained ghost has been seen, stomping up and down this corridor, pulling at the dagger in his chest. And wailing like you'd never believe.'

Ellie's wonderful tale had the desired effect.

'I've . . . just remembered . . .' Mrs Fadget's voice was so frightened she was stumbling over her words. 'I have to go this other way and have no need to pass that door after all.'

And we heard her wooden pattens clattering away from us.

Ellie appeared at the corner.

'Well done,' I cried. 'Mr Somers himself could not have told a better story.'

'And Mr Somers could not have picked a lock more cleanly,' declared Masou.

He stood up, turned the handle and flung open the door to the workshop. We slipped inside and closed it behind us.

'I am indeed multi-talented,' Masou continued. 'Not only the Queen's favourite fool and the best tumbler in Mr Somers's troupe but an expert burglar to boot. I believe I—'

He stopped as a cloth hit him in the face. 'That's enough from you, Master Housebreaker,' growled Ellie.

I had a good look around. The workshop was unchanged from when I had last been here two days ago. Except of course, poor Mr Urseau's body was now lying in the crypt of St Mary's Church in

Hampton village. Only a dull bloodstain remained to show us where he had lain. The windows gave some light but Masou produced a tinder box and lit the candles for us.

'We are looking for something that would fit a small key,' I said.

'And I would like nothing better than to stay and help you,' said Masou. 'But there is a thirsty troupe waiting for their beer and I have annoyed them enough today.' He made for the door. 'I wish you luck, although there are so many keyholes here that it might be like finding a grain of rice in a desert full of sand.'

'Yet if Ellie is right and his last words were "the key"—' I began.

'I am,' Ellie put in.

'Then it is likely we will find our answer here,' I finished.

Masou bowed again, gave us a cheeky smile and went on his way.

To my surprise Ellie climbed on a chair and tested the windows. Then she jumped on each slab on the floor.

'What are you doing?' I asked.

'I'm making sure there's no secret ways into the room,' she told me as she tapped the walls and listened. Suddenly she shivered and looked over her shoulder.

'What ails you, Ellie?' I asked.

'I remembered Mr Urseau's gory ghost,' she said in a hushed voice. 'He might appear behind me at any moment, wailing and rattling his chains.'

'But *you* made that story up,' I said. 'There is no ghost.'

Ellie glanced nervously into the furthest corner from the candlelight. 'There *could* be,' she whispered. 'He might be walking this very room to find his murderer. Oh, I wish I had some basil or my elf-shot for protection.'

I gave her a hug. 'There is nothing to be scared of,' I said. 'If the clockmaker should walk, he would know that we are trying to help and would not seek to frighten us.'

'Maybe,' muttered Ellie, but she kept glancing around nervously.

I began to examine the clocks and tools on the shelves. The clocks were of all sizes and in different states of repair. Some had their workings scattered about them. The springs and cogs made the whole business look very complicated.

Then I made an exciting discovery. Tucked behind some ledgers was a wooden letter-box just as the widow had described — about the size of a large Bible. I felt my pulse quicken. I grasped it and tried to open the lid. It was locked.

'Look at this, Ellie,' I said eagerly as I held it out.

'I think the keyhole's too big for the key that was in Mr Urseau's hand.' Ellie peered at it, frowning.

'I agree,' I said. 'But I am sure this is the box that Mrs Urseau seeks — it may contain the treasure. We should take it to her — however, there is no harm in us looking inside first. There must be a key for it somewhere.'

We ferreted about the shelves and worktables.

'Found some!' cried Ellie, holding up a ring with a dozen keys on it.

'Try them,' I urged her.

We tried each key twice, but none fitted.

'By my troth!' I exclaimed. 'We have a box with no key and a key with no keyhole. This mystery just gets deeper and deeper. Hide the box under your apron, Ellie. It is time we left this place. We can try to open the box back in my chamber. Mayhap Masou can help again.'

Making sure that the passage was empty, we slipped out, Ellie cradling her heavy burden and walking as if she had a bellyache. I pulled the door

shut, but of course I could not lock it. I went back in and found Mr Urseau's door key still hanging on the hook where Charles had pointed it out. I joined Ellie and locked the door.

We were lucky to find my bedchamber empty. Sarah must still have been 'sitting quietly, thinking' somewhere and the other Maids were obviously fully entranced with the archers. I put the box on my bed.

'We need fetch Masou again,' I said to Ellie. 'He may have finished his practice now.'

'We don't need him!' Ellie declared. 'Let me have a go.' She picked up a hairpin from the table, fiddled with the lock for a while and then threw the hairpin down. 'No, this bends too easily.' She rummaged through my jewellery and hair things. 'This will do the trick,' she announced, unfastening the pin of a brooch.

I waited a few minutes while she wiggled the pin sideways, tongue stuck out in concentration. 'Desist, Ellie,' I laughed. 'You have given it a fair go – now let's find Masou.'

'Hmmm,' she said. 'I'll go.' She was gone for about ten minutes and came back alone.

'Where is he?' I asked.

'I couldn't find him and then I had a better idea.' Ellie smiled. She pulled out a large kitchen knife from under her apron.

'God's Oath!' I cried. 'What are you about?'

'I'll have to work fast,' said Ellie. 'Mr Friar will swing a ladle at me if he knows I've taken it.'

She advanced upon the box. I wondered if she had bothered to try and find Masou at all, so determined did she seem to open this box herself.

'Stop!' I cried. 'We cannot take it to Mrs Urseau if it is damaged. It is her property after all, as the widow. We could never explain that we've had a good look inside.'

I was too late. Ellie had already slipped the blade between the lid and the box. She moved it back and forth but nothing happened. I snatched the box from her.

'Enough!' I said. 'We will find Masou later. Now help me get ready, for it is almost supper.'

I shoved the box firmly under my pillow.

A few minutes later

I had to stop for a moment. My eyelids are

growing very heavy and I must sleep soon. I cannot afford to have another sleepless night. I might fall down in front of the Court tomorrow and start snoring! That would certainly not please Her Majesty. But I must finish the account of what happened today.

Supper was delicious. Mr Friar, who did not seem to have noticed his missing knife, had made his chicken with lemons, a recipe of his own devising. He knows that the Queen is fond of it. I think everyone enjoyed it – except perhaps Mrs Urseau, who was there as a special guest of the Queen in honour of her late husband's loyal service. She seemed not to notice what she ate – though I doubted that was from grief. I made sure that I sat opposite her in case anything interesting was discussed.

Mrs Urseau soon fixed her neighbours with a question: 'Have any of you heard tell of a box that would have been in my husband's possession?' she said eagerly. 'It is mine now, of course – indeed, I have the key that will fit it.'

The courtiers about her expressed interest but none had heard of it. I sat there feeling very guilty. It had to be the box that I had found in the workshop and was now hidden under my pillow. Faith, I had become a thief! I wondered what Mr Hatton would think if he had to march *me* off to prison. He would probably be glad to be rid of a meddlesome Maid!

'My husband's will left everything to me,' the widow went on. 'Everything except for his favourite clock, which he left to Charles Doute.'

'The clock may also be yours now,' I said, 'if Charles is found guilty of your husband's murder.'

'I never cared for it.' Mrs Urseau was dismissive in her tone. 'Or any of the clocks for that matter. Charles is welcome to it — much good it will do him where he's going! I just want my due: the money my husband was squirreling away all these years.'

I was even more certain that the box would have the treasure in it — and its contents could be a clue to his murder. Had Mr Urseau been rich? His widow certainly hoped so. Did this give her the motive to kill him? She seemed desperate to get hold of the box and is clearly not moved by her husband's death. Mrs Urseau had just become my next suspect.

God's Bodkin! I have just jerked awake, quill still in

my hand. Fortunately there is no ink on the sheets. Tomorrow I hope to discover what is in the box, but for now I must move it from under my pillow to under my bed so that I can get some sleep. And, oddly, that terrible smell seems to be getting worse.

The Twenty-eighth Day of September, in the Year of Our Lord 1570

Before breakfast

I woke this morning with an even stronger whiff of that strange odour that seems to permeate the air. Faugh! It quite overpowers Lady Sarah's lotions and potions. Groggily, I determined to figure out where it is coming from and put a stop to it.

But soon I thought I was still dreaming, for I saw a vision of Ellie creeping around my chamber with a large hammer! Then, horror of horrors, she came towards me with a wild look in her eyes. I sat bolt upright and blinked hard. Ellie was still there.

'What are you about?' I hissed.

'That box!' muttered Ellie through gritted teeth. 'I won't be beaten by it. This ought to get it open.'

She stepped up to my bed, pulled out the box and raised the hammer right over it.

'No, Ellie!' I whispered urgently. 'If we have to show it to Mrs Urseau smashed to pieces, she will accuse us of robbery. And besides,' I added, pointing to the slumbering Mary Shelton and Sarah, 'they will think you have gone woodwild!'

Ellie reluctantly put the hammer down. She glared at the box for a moment, then snatched it up and tried to dig her nails under the lid.

'Ellie! That is enough!'

My tiring woman nodded crossly as I swung my legs over the side of the bed to get up. As soon as she thought I was not looking, she took hold of one corner of the box in her teeth and tried to wrench the lid up. I grabbed at it, and for a moment we were like a dog and its master pulling at a stick. I am sure I heard her growl!

'Faith!' I said, keeping my voice low. 'Henri would be proud of that performance. But you must stop now, Ellie. We shall seek out Masou. He is the only one who can help us open the thing without losing teeth or nails.' I thrust the box into her hands. 'Now go and find him — and promise you will not try any more silly ways to get it open.'

'Very well then,' muttered my friend. 'But what if we dropped it off the roof?'

'No!'

'Or got one of the pigs to sit on it?'

'NO!'

'Then it'll have to be Masou,' sniffed Ellie, with
a toss of her head. 'Seems a waste of time to me,
getting him, but—' She shrugged and flounced off.

Now Sarah and Mary are stirring. My stomach
is telling me to dress quickly for breakfast, but as I
have not got Ellie to help me, I shall have ask
Olwen before Sarah needs her.

I hope Ellie leaves the box alone while I am
gone. I shall be forced to have one of the pigs sit
on her if she does not!

After breakfast, in my bedchamber

I am now almost as cross with this wretched box as
Ellie is! I returned to my bedchamber after
breakfast to find it waiting for me – clutched in
her fevered hands. I was relieved to see she had not
jumped on it or been at it with a saw.

'So much for Masou,' she sniffed, dumping the
box on my bed. 'He says he can scarce get a
toothpick in that stupid lock, let alone turn it.
What did I tell you, Grace? Now, where did I put
that hammer . . . ?'

'We will have none of that, dear Ellie,' I said

firmly, taking her by the arm. 'I promise, I am as anxious as you to see the contents, and we shall soon enough.'

'Can't think how.' Ellie was not to be appeased. 'Unless we stand here till it pops itself open by magic.'

'There is an easier way,' I told her. 'We shall take it to Mrs Urseau. If she is as eager as she says to see the contents, she will open it in front of us. We shall find a time as soon as I am free.'

'Yes, well,' muttered Ellie. 'That might work, I suppose.'

Now she is taking out her crossness on one of my petticoats, giving it a violent shaking. I hope we can find time to see Mrs Urseau today. I may be able to determine in my mind whether she had anything to do with her husband's death. And anyway, Ellie will burst if the box is not opened soon!

Early afternoon

Heavens be praised! Her Majesty is deep in political business of some sort with her close advisers – all day! I know I should not be pleased that she has such boring tasks, but it has given me a good chance to continue with my investigations. I have found out two important things today and have come to a quiet corner in the Great Hall, where I will not be disturbed while I write them down.

As soon as we had breakfasted, Mrs Champernowne bustled up.

'Take your embroidery, look you, girls,' she said to all the Maids, 'and sit down quiet and ladylike in the Presence Chamber. Her Majesty is still displeased with you.' Here she glared at Lady Jane. 'We do not want her to overhear any more silly gossip about murder now, do we?'

Silly gossip. That was rich! I had heard Mrs Champernowne exchanging eager whispers on the very same subject with Fran and Olwen in our bedchamber earlier.

Jane pouted and I felt a little guilty that I had got her into trouble. The pity is, she will never know that it was all in a good cause. (At least I *hope* it is in a good cause. As I write, the mystery is not yet solved.)

I thought it was to be a very quiet, very boring

morning under the watchful eye of the Queen. Her displeasure can make the warmest day turn icy! But when we arrived at the door to the Presence Chamber, we were greeted with the excellent news that the Queen was so busy wading through matters of State that she forbade us from attending her. I could hardly hide my delight. I would fetch Ellie and go to Mrs Urseau without delay, before Mrs Champernowne got it into her head that this would be a good time for more dancing lessons with Monsieur Danton!

However, Lady Sarah had other plans. She tucked her arm firmly in mine.

'Dear Grace,' she said in a wheedling tone as we all made for our bedchambers, 'I am so glad we are free. I have a new sonnet sent me by Mr Cheshire. Please read it with me and tell me what you think – for you have such a love of words.'

My heart sank to my slippers. I knew what that meant. Every phrase would be examined minutely, and if Mr Cheshire had not compared my beauteous lady to a flower, the sun and the stars at least ten times each, she would think he had found another love and sink into misery.

Mary must have seen the look of panic on my face, for she came to my rescue. 'You are in great demand this morning, Grace!' she laughed. 'Do you not remember the handkerchief that I am making as a present for my father? I am all behind and you promised you would help as soon as you could. I must lay first claim to you.'

'Ah, yes,' I said with a grateful look to my rescuer. 'Silly me. How could I have forgotten? I am sorry, Sarah. I would love to read your sonnet and will do so as soon as I can.'

I thought Sarah might be cross, but luck was on my side, for Daniel Cheshire himself appeared on the horizon and she promptly vanished from our side. I am hoping not to bump into her for the rest of the day!

'Thank you, Mary,' I said as soon as she was out of earshot. 'You have saved me a good deal of torment. One of Daniel's sonnets is much like the others. There is more passion than poetry in them – though I would not say that to our love-struck Sarah.'

Mary gave me a quizzical stare. 'Get you gone!' she said. 'I hope that whatever you have to do is worth my little white lie!'

'It is!' I said with a grin, and rushed off.

Mary is truly amazing! She is the only one of the Maids who has any inkling about my secret work. And yet she says nothing to anyone and does not ask me any questions. I am sure I could not keep quiet if I were her. I am much too nosy!'

Ellie and I were soon on our way to Mrs Urseau's cottage. Ellie carried the box, wrapped carefully in a cloth.

'I know that woman is a bossy old baggage,' she said, 'but do you really think she killed her own husband?'

'I cannot ignore the possibility,' I replied as we walked together through the Base Court. 'She is desperate for his money, and perhaps she decided that murdering him was the only way to get it.'

'I just can't for the life of me think how she could have managed it,' said Ellie. 'He was killed in a locked room—'

'She could have a workshop key of her own that Charles didn't know about,' I reasoned. 'But then, even if she did, we would surely have seen her fleeing.' I sighed. 'Oh dear, now I am pointing the finger at Charles again. This will not do. We must at least find out where the widow was when the clockmaker was done to death.'

Mrs Urseau seemed even less pleased to see us than before. We soon saw why. Her room was strewn with her belongings and there were trunks and baskets lying about, half packed.

'I shall be returning to my family in Somerset tomorrow,' she told us as she piled some clothes into one of the trunks. 'There is no future for me at Court now that my husband is dead. Not that I ever got much from living here,' she added with a sniff. 'I'll be glad to go.'

So she was not even going to wait to see her husband buried. Was this the callous action of a murderer?

'I know some will wonder why I do not attend my own husband's funeral,' she said, 'but I fear it would be too trying for me.'

I thought it was more likely that she was angry at her husband for not leaving her his treasure.

'I hope that, in your new life, you will be able to banish the dreadful day of your husband's death from your mind,' I said, hoping to work my way round to discovering where she was at that crucial time. It was tricky to interview someone who did not know they were a suspect.

'I doubt it,' she said, straightening up sharply and banging the lid down. 'To think I set off for market that day with not a thought of the news that would greet me when I returned. There was I, talking to Seth Oakham about some fine eggs he had brought to sell, and back at the palace my husband was lying with a dagger in his chest.'

This sounded honest enough, although I knew that clever murderers used the utmost cunning to cover their tracks, and Mrs Urseau was clearly not a stupid woman.

'Anyhow,' she went on, 'as you can see, I'm busy and have no one to help—'

I saw Ellie back away at this. I hurriedly took the box from her and removed its cloth cover. Mrs Urseau's mouth dropped open. She made a grab for it and cradled it like a baby.

'Where did you get this?' she demanded.

I would have to be careful how I answered.

'Mr Hatton takes great pains in his investigations,' I told her. 'He gathers together everything that he thinks is important in finding the truth.'

'So you got it from him,' said Mrs Urseau.

I smiled. Well, I had not told a lie. I could not help it if Mrs Urseau had come to the wrong conclusion.

'I am sure the Captain of the Guard will be eager to hear what you find inside,' I hinted.

There was an awkward silence. Mrs Urseau stroked the lid of the box lovingly but made no move to open it. It seemed she intended to wait until we were gone before she viewed its contents. I would have to see about that! I wobbled dramatically and dropped onto the end of the bench – the one that was free of tin plates and tankards.

'I am feeling rather strange,' I said in a weak voice. 'I fear we cannot depart yet. The sun is fierce and I may faint as soon as I step outside. But please do not let me stop you going about your business, Mrs Urseau.'

Ellie raised her eyebrows at me. She knows I am as likely to faint as fly to the moon, but she came over and dutifully flapped a hand at me to cool me down. The widow just stood looking at us, no doubt waiting for me to recover and leave. How was I ever going to get her to open her box? I cast around for more excuses to stay.

'Thank you, I feel a little better now,' I said after a while. 'But . . . this hot weather has given me such a thirst.'

I could see that Mrs Urseau was struggling to hide her impatience with me as she poured something out of a pitcher that stood on the table. 'There's a sip of apple juice in there,' she said, handing a glass to me. 'I've no more for I'll soon be gone.'

I drank as slowly as I could but there was so

little in the glass that I had soon finished.

'It is a beautiful box,' I tried next. 'I hope you find what you wish within it.'

'So do I,' said Mrs Urseau. 'Now, if you've finished . . .'

This was getting me nowhere! It was time for a more direct approach.

'Why do you not look inside?' I went on. 'I confess I am most anxious to see that you have not been left penniless. If that is the case, I could speak to the Queen on your behalf—'

This was too much for the clockmaker's widow. She put the box down on the table, turned and plunged her hand into a deep bowl on a shelf, pulling out a bunch of keys. I could see that her fingers were trembling as she chose a small one and inserted it in the lock. But was it the nervousness of an innocent woman, or that of a murderer about to reap her ill-gotten rewards? I crept up behind her. Ellie was soon with me, nudging me hard in the ribs in her excitement.

There did not appear to be anything valuable in the box – only boring papers squashed in together. But to my surprise Mrs Urseau did not seem at all disappointed. She pulled them out and spread them over the table, riffling through with eager fingers.

She cast aside complicated drawings of clock workings and receipts for tools that her husband had purchased, and at last saw what she was looking for. She gathered a bunch of papers up and spun round so suddenly that we hardly had the chance to jump back. Fortunately Mrs Urseau was too bound up in what she had found to notice that we had been breathing down her neck.

'I knew it! Promissory notes!' she said in triumph. I would not have gone so far as to call that treasure, but gossip at Court was always exaggerated. She flicked through them quickly. 'When I get all the money that's owed to my husband in these, there'll be enough to see me comfortable for a good while.'

She gathered the papers together, put them firmly back in the box and locked it.

'Perhaps I shall bide a few more days here and call in the debts,' she said, and for the first time I thought I saw the flicker of a smile on her hard features. It was soon gone though. 'This money will serve me well, but if only all this had happened a few months later.'

I did not know what to say, and I suppose my confusion showed, for she went on to explain: 'I could have had at least twice this if Nicholas had died after his father – the old man is better off than us, and if he had gone first, this would have been an even bigger inheritance. As it is, I shall have nothing from him.'

I had never before seen a woman so intent on her husband's money. Not only did his death not seem to move her at all, but she was even complaining about the timing!

Still, no matter how distasteful her character, all this new information led to the conclusion that she would not have wanted her husband dead. It was unlikely, then, that I would find she was involved in the murder.

'You will be able to attend your husband's funeral as well,' I could not resist saying as Ellie and I took our leave. We did not wait for an answer.

As we left the room, I realized that this was another perfect reason not to be married, and always to stay at Court with Her Majesty.

'This mystery baffles me still,' I said to Ellie on our way back. 'But I still have one item on my list to investigate – otherwise I will have to conclude that Charles was indeed the murderer. But I just have this feeling in my gut that he is innocent.'

'That'll be 'cos you're hungry,' Ellie retorted. 'As usual!'

I would have chased her all over the palace – if there had not been so many courtiers around. I do not see why it is so unseemly for a fifteen-year-old Maid of Honour to be seen running, but there it is.

I didn't really mind her teasing, and soon I was back to thinking about the murder. Two of my three leads – the meetings and the treasure had been fully investigated. Now I had to put all my efforts into speaking with Jem Ainsworth.

I was totally lost in thought when we came round a corner and bumped straight into Masou. Well, he bumped into us – the silly boy was practising his somersaults and not looking where he was going. He made a great play of hopping up and down on the flagstones, holding his foot and declaring that we had broken all his bones and he would never walk again.

'By Shaitan, you two are a jinx on me!' he groaned. 'Is there no part of the palace that is safe from you?'

'Stow it, Masou!' laughed Ellie. She gave him a shove that sent him into an elegant cartwheel, proving there was nothing wrong with his foot at all. 'It would take a charging boar to do you any damage.'

'I would sooner face a boar than the fiends I see before me.' Masou grinned, skipping round us as if keeping a safe distance. 'And speaking of boars – I have just come from the kitchen and seen a very fine one.' He chuckled. 'Not roasting on a spit, but sitting on a stool.'

'For Heaven's sake, Masou,' I said. 'You are not making witty jests for the Queen now. Explain yourself in plain words.'

'It is Jem Ainsworth,' Masou told us, puffing out his cheeks in a good imitation of a fat braggart. 'And if he does not cease his everlasting stories about the clockmaker, he will be the biggest *bore* the kitchen has ever seen.'

We groaned at the pun.

'His tales have become so ridiculous,' Masou went on. 'He would have the servants believe that the hapless victim died at the hands of invisible fairy brigands! And as I left, he was telling of a mysterious package that he delivered to Mr Urseau.'

My ears pricked up. 'Mysterious package? Did he say any more?'

Masou shrugged. 'I warrant he told his audience that it was a box of goblins, but I left and did not hear it.'

'Why did you not tell us of the package in the first place?' I picked up my skirts. 'Come, Ellie. We must go to the kitchen!'

We left Masou scratching his head, and ran. I did not care if I was seen running and was later chided by Mrs Champernowne. I needed to hear what Jem Ainsworth had to say! (At the time of writing this, Mrs Champernowne has said nothing to me so I must have got away with it.)

We reached the kitchen and—

Early evening, before supper

So much for not being disturbed! Lady Sarah found me — I do not know how, for I thought I was well hidden. She was about to read her sonnet to Carmina and Lucy. (For the fifth time, Carmina whispered to me!) So I had to endure the reading and leave off writing my account until now.

The sonnet was as dreadful as I expected. I only managed to escape by telling Sarah that I needed to go up to my bedchamber to write down such a beautiful poem in my daybooke. A lie, I am afraid. I would not sully these pages with such nonsense!

But now I can get back to the interesting events in the kitchen this afternoon.

I feel as if I am at least close to solving this perplexing puzzle. If Jem Ainsworth were not so fat and smelly, I could kiss him! He proved to be most entertaining with his tall tales. He also gave me a wonderful lead in this mystery – although he had no idea that he had done so.

Ellie and I found Mr Ainsworth exactly where Masou had said, sitting by the fire and stuffing his jowls with food left from the noontide meal. There was a lull in the work of the kitchen between dinner and supper and he had an appreciative audience in the kitchen staff. They had all gathered around him, from Mr Friar to the spitboy. I feared he might stop talking when he saw us approach, but his face lit up. The servants all jumped to their feet.

'I am honoured,' he said. 'A new pair of ears is always welcome, but one of Her Majesty's Maids – well, I'm quite overcome.'

'I pray that everyone will sit down and pay no heed to me,' I said. 'Please continue with your story, Mr Ainsworth. I am especially keen to hear of the package you delivered to the poor clockmaker.'

'My lady goes straight to the heart of the matter.' He looked smug and self-important, but I did not mind that. I had that funny feeling again and it was not hunger, no matter what Ellie might say. I was sure that the package was important in the mystery. Jem took another swig of small beer, burped and then continued.

'It were a clock,' he announced proudly.

I sensed an air of disappointment run through the listening kitchen servants. A clock being delivered to the clockmaker did not sound exciting to them at all.

'A broken clock?' I prompted him.

'Not at all,' he said. 'It were brought by a special messenger and were a gift to the Queen from Lord Sheringham himself.'

'Of course.' Mr Friar nodded. 'Mr Urseau would never let Her Majesty receive such a gift without checking that it worked properly.'

'What did the clock look like?' I asked.

Jem shook his head, making his jowls wobble. 'I dunno. It were all wrapped up in a cloth with a parchment attached. But it were big. Nearly as tall as me, and very heavy. It were too much for me on my own to carry. I had to put it on a cart to get it through the passageways to the workshop.'

He stood up and made a dumb show of how he'd panted and heaved the clock onto the cart. The servants loved it.

'What was on the parchment?' I said. 'Was it a message?'

'I couldn't say, my lady,' he said with a shrug, 'for I can't read. Mr Urseau were stood in his chamber and I could see he had the look of death on him.' The porter continued with his tale, but he had now entered the world of his own imagination. We would learn nothing more here. But that did not matter, for I had a strong notion about what had really happened to the poor clockmaker.

I thanked him, and Ellie and I took our leave.

'You're excited about something, Grace,' panted Ellie as she struggled to keep up with me. I had a purpose and was walking as quickly as my skirts would allow.

'I believe that the clock is important in our mystery,' I told her eagerly. 'It was delivered just before Mr Urseau was killed. We must have a look at it.' I stopped in my tracks and turned to face her. 'Do you not see, Ellie? Jem Ainsworth said it was very big and very heavy. It could be that an assassin with a dagger was hiding *inside* it, ready to strike the Queen. But Mr Urseau was the first to examine the clock. He took the key that was later found clutched in his hand, opened the clock and found the assassin. It leads back to attempted treason: Mr Urseau was not the intended victim. Indeed, Mr Urseau should have been catching up on his sleep after his nocturnal dancing and not at his workshop at all. It was only his duty to examine the Queen's gift that took him there.'

'That's horrible,' said Ellie with a shudder. 'He was silenced before he could raise the alarm.'

I felt a thrill at finally coming upon such a lead: a possible scenario for how the murder could take place in a locked room! But as we hurried along, another thought came into my head that spoiled everything.

'Ellie!' I wailed. 'If there had been an assassin lurking in the clock, then where did he go after he killed Mr Urseau?'

She looked at me blankly.

'The assassin would have had to stab Mr Urseau, unlock the door, lock it again and escape before we all arrived. Remember – it was just moments after we heard the cry that we reached the workshop.'

'And we saw no one running away and there

was only the one way out.' Ellie nodded. 'It still comes back to Charles, Grace.'

Not for the first time, I wondered if I was running around after a mystery that did not exist. I was beginning to feel like a cat chasing its own tail! But I could not help clinging to the idea of Charles's innocence. And then I had another thought.

'Unless the assassin hid back inside the clock,' I exclaimed.

Ellie gave a shudder. 'Then he would have been there the whole time we were,' she said quietly. 'When Mr Urseau was murdered – and maybe even when we found the box.'

I looked at her. 'He might be there still.'

Ellie shook her head. 'But it's been days since—'

'The workshop was crawling with people soon after Mr Urseau was murdered,' I pointed out. 'And Mr Hatton had it locked when the corpse was removed. Mayhap our fiend had no choice but to stay in the workshop, waiting for a chance to sneak out undetected. And he cannot have known about Mr Urseau's door key, for that was still inside when we went back.'

'Be sensible, Grace,' said Ellie. 'Even if he *was* in the clock, no one could put up with being stuffed into such a small space for so long.'

'I agree,' I replied. 'But with the workshop locked and no one going there except us, he has a whole room to himself. It is fanciful, I warrant, but . . . Ellie, the murderer may still be here at Hampton Court!'

We were walking so fast, we were almost at the workshop now. Ellie began to hang back. I guessed what she was thinking.

'We *have* to do this, Ellie,' I said. 'There are two of us and only one assassin.'

'Shouldn't we get Masou?' Ellie was white. 'Or one of the Gentlemen Guard?'

'We cannot,' I told her. 'The matter is closed as far as Mr Hatton is concerned. He would not allow his Gentlemen Guards to accompany us on such a fool's errand. And we've pilfered enough of Masou's time today.'

'Wait a minute, then.' Ellie suddenly vanished down the passageway towards the carpenters' workshop. She was soon back with a length of wood. 'Let the murderer try something now!' she said, swishing it fiercely over her head like a broadsword.

I pulled the key to the workshop out of my purse and turned it in the lock.

'One, two, three!' I said. I pushed the door wide open.

'Come on out, you villain,' called Ellie, 'and feel the edge of my . . . plank!'

Nothing moved. We went in slowly and glanced around. There was only one clock big enough to fit Jem's description. It was not the clock itself that was big, but the cabinet fixed beneath it. I had not noticed it before. I stepped towards it, holding up my skirts as I trod around the bloodstain on the floor, even though it was long dry.

'Careful, Grace,' whispered Ellie, waving her length of wood about.

The cabinet was indeed big enough for a man to hide in. It was a beautiful piece of work, with an inlaid Tudor rose on the panelling. I peered at every inch of the wood but I could not find a gap or a hinge or a handle that would give away the door.

'There is no way in,' I said in disappointment. 'I cannot see how a man could get inside.'

'Then there's no assassin lurking in there waiting to kill us?' said Ellie, hopeful.

I shook my head and she put down her wood with a clatter. 'But that means we still don't know what happened,' I said. Yet something about this clock had led to Mr Urseau's death – I was certain of it. And it struck me as strange that the clock needed so large a cabinet beneath.

Then I saw a piece of parchment on a shelf next to the clock. It had to be the one Jem Ainsworth had talked of.

'Look at this, Ellie,' I said eagerly and smoothed it out.

It was a message for the Queen.

'*My Most Royal and Gracious Majesty, I give to you this humble token of my loyalty,*' I read out loud. '*The E on the clock face is for our glorious Queen Elizabeth.*'

'There it is,' cried Ellie, pointing up at the clock face. 'That's one letter I do know. E for Ellie.'

'Yes,' I agreed. 'This is the clock.' It was a beautiful timepiece. The face had engravings of the sun and the moon on either side of the beautiful E. The end of the hand was a small E fashioned out of the metal. The whole face was covered with a glass case. I read on: '*If the hand is set to twelve o'clock, it will reveal a delight for the heart of Our Beloved Sovereign.*'

'I wonder what it could be,' pondered Ellie, standing on tiptoe to examine the face of the clock closely.

'Let us see,' I said, and went to open the glass case covering the hand. But it was locked. There was a tiny keyhole in the wood beside the face. I ran my finger over it. 'I can guess which key opens this. The one that Mr Hatton holds in his possession at this very moment!'

'The one that Mr Urseau used his dying breath to tell us about,' gasped Ellie.

I was not going to get into another argument about the clockmaker's last words.

'If the keyhole on Mrs Urseau's box defeated Masou, then he will have no chance with this,' I said. 'It is even smaller. There is only one thing for it. We have to get the key from Mr Hatton somehow.'

'I can just see you going up and asking him for it,' giggled Ellie. 'And he'll say, "Why, of course, Lady Grace, here it is"!'

'There must be another way,' I said, and I began to make my plans.

After supper, before bed time

I have never been so uncomfortable making an

entry in my daybooke. I am in my bed, but so is Ellie, so I only have a quarter of the space I am used to. She has an elbow digging into my ribs and is snoring in my ear! My thoughts are tumbling around (much like Ellie) after what I have discovered. I will write quickly and then catch up on my sleep – I hope!

As I went into supper, I saw that Mr Somers's troupe was going to entertain us while we ate. This was perfect. I caught Masou's eye and winked at him to let him know I wanted a word. He had barely nodded to me when I had to duck down behind Mary Shelton. Monsieur Danton had suddenly popped up nearby. I did not want to arrange another dancing lesson. No sooner had he gone past than I saw Lady Sarah approaching, flapping a piece of vellum. Not another poem! Did Mr Cheshire have nothing better to do with his time than write twaddle for my lady? Mr Hatton does not work his Gentleman Guards hard enough, in my opinion!

I grabbed Mary by the arm and hurried her through the crowd. I made sure I sat her between Sarah and me.

And then I got a dreadful shock, for this meant I was sitting opposite Mr Stephen Morling! Luckily he had no more wish to speak with me than I with him – and certainly not about secret dancing. We just eyed each other in embarrassment and got on with our venison. To the relief of us both, he soon found himself being talked at earnestly by Lady Jane. She was his neighbour and seemed desperate to engage him in conversation.

'Mr Morling!' she said firmly. 'How are you finding the meal? Is it not the best you have ever tasted?'

Mr Morling looked very pleased and went quite pink as he replied. I hope he never discovers that Jane was talking to him simply to avoid Sir Thomas Cartwright. Sir Thomas had made a beeline to sit by her side, only to find her back turned against him. Now I think about it, it is quite funny that, on the one hand, Jane was trying to shake off a suitor and, on the other, Lady Sarah was positively obsessed with hers. And as if she had heard my thoughts, my lovesick lady reached across Mary and grabbed my sleeve.

'Listen to this, Grace,' she said. 'Listen to what Mr Cheshire says about my eyes.' And off she went in a dreamy voice:

> *'My heart like a running hart leaps,*
> *And a strange feeling o'er me doth creep.*
> *It goeth from my head to my toes*
> *When I behold Sarah, my blooming rose.'*

I was not sure whether to vomit up my venison or fall from my chair laughing. Why do young men lose all their sense when they are in love? And why must I hear it? Now I have sullied my pages with his verse, when I swore not to! Fie upon you, Mr Cheshire.

Fortunately I was saved from any more as we got up to go to the Banqueting House for dessert. I managed to get between Carmina and Lucy and join their conversation about slippers or something. (I was not paying attention.)

As soon as we were in the Banqueting House I went to seek out Masou. I found him taking an egg out of Sir Pelham Poucher's ear. Sir Pelham was sitting in the nearest seat to the food, with a huge platter of jumbals in his hand. I hoped he had left some – I love the ring-shaped biscuits. I used to thread them onto my fingers like rings when I was little – before I reached an age when such behaviour became 'unseemly'.

'Lady Grace,' said Masou when he saw me, 'what

is that I see on your hat?' I bent forward for him to look. 'Now, what did you want the great Masou for?' he whispered, producing a jumbal from the brim and handing it to me.

I looked around. Only Sir Pelham was within earshot and he was busy with his biscuits – plus he is deaf, to boot. In between mouthfuls, I told Masou about the clock we had discovered and how I thought it held a clue to the murder.

'So I will need you to come with me to the workshop to inspect this clock when everyone else is asleep,' I muttered. 'But there is one problem. The clock face is locked and I believe its key is the very one that Mr Urseau was clutching in his hand. The one that Mr Hatton now keeps securely in the pouch on his belt.'

Masou gave an overdramatic sigh and tutted. 'By Allah,' he said teasingly, 'you cannot do without me, my lady. You need me to help the key "leap" from Mr Hatton's belt into your hand. Nothing could be simpler. Mayhap I shall do it for the whole Court to see. There would be much applause.'

I opened my mouth to protest about this ridiculous idea (which I was almost certain he would not really think of doing), but Masou was too quick. Before I knew it, he was springing from the back of Sir Pelham's chair and over the heads of several surprised courtiers to land next to Mr Hatton. The Captain of the Guard was standing with some of the Queen's councillors. I moved closer and watched intently, worries starting to worm round my brain. Supposing Masou were caught! I had not given a thought to the danger he might be in. Even my clever friend could make mistakes after all – though he would never admit it. Stealing from Mr Hatton would be a serious crime. I knew I would never forgive myself if he were found out.

If I had not been so worried, the surprised look on Mr Hatton's face as Masou dropped down right next to him would have sent me into fits of laughter. But he recovered his dignity very quickly. Mr Hatton is a serious man who does not have much time for japes – especially when they come from the Queen's favourite fool.

But Masou was not beaten. He put on a charming – or rather, idiotic – smile and apologized. 'I could not help but come and admire your beautiful flowers, sir,' he gushed.

Mr Hatton looked irritated at this fresh piece of nonsense. I must admit I wondered where it was leading.

'What the—?' was all he could manage before Masou produced a beautiful bunch of chrysanthemums, seemingly from Mr Hatton's sleeve. Everyone around gasped and clapped as he handed them to the Captain of the Guard, who looked as if he felt rather silly standing there clutching his posy. Masou skipped off to tumble elsewhere, with a secret wave to me as he went. He must have done the deed — although I could not see how.

At that moment Queen came over, and everyone bowed and curtsied.

'A happy lady indeed,' she said to Mr Hatton with a twinkle in her eye, 'and beautiful to be thus honoured by such a beautiful gift. Who are they for, sir? Or is it a secret?'

I am sure the Queen was teasing the poor man, who looked most uncomfortable. It is well known that Mr Hatton thinks the world of the Queen, and never looks at another woman. And if Her Majesty *really* thought her Captain of the Guard had found a new love, she would not be smiling.

But Mr Hatton is a quick-witted man. He made the most of the occasion by kneeling in front of the Queen and presenting her with the flowers.

'There is only one lady whose beauty matches these blooms,' he mumbled.

The Queen loves a surprise gift – even when it is one she is fully expecting – and she thanked Mr Hatton as if it were the most precious thing she had ever received.

A little while later, Masou tumbled back in my direction and gave me a wink. 'Meet me tonight at the workshop,' I whispered to him, before he danced across the room to entertain the Queen.

A thought has occurred to me. I wonder where Masou got the flowers from. Perhaps he filched them from Daniel Cheshire. Mr Cheshire brings flowers for his love every day. At least, that is what Sarah tells us. I must find out from her if he missed a delivery. On second thought, no – I would be sonneted to death!

As soon as Ellie came to help me get ready for bed, I told her of my plan to go with Masou and find out the secret of the clock. We spoke in whispers, so as not to wake Mary Shelton. Lady Sarah had not come up to bed yet. I expect she could not tear herself away from Mr Cheshire. It was a moonlit night, so no doubt there will soon be a flood of terrible poems on the subject!

Ellie raised her eyes to the Heavens at the mention of my plan. 'I s'pose I'm to go trailing along with you,' she sighed. 'When I've only just got over the last night-time adventure you took me on – and with no chance of a dance this time.'

'I have something much more important for you to do,' I told her.

'Gawd help me!' groaned Ellie. She wagged her finger at me. 'Now if you think I'm going off on my own, Grace, you've got another—'

I caught her hand. 'Dear Ellie, I would not think of such a thing.' I put on a mock solemn face. 'But what I ask will be difficult. I am not certain that you will be able to do it.'

'Bet I can,' said Ellie, offended. 'What is it?'

I laughed and patted the bed. 'I need you to stay here, under these covers, and pretend to be me so that no one will know I am gone!'

Ellie's face broke into a broad grin. 'Why didn't you say so, then?' she chuckled. 'I'll play Lady Grace to the life. And make sure you're not back before morning. Your bed's much more comfortable than mine.'

'Thank you, Ellie. I shall do my best,' I assured her.

'You better take my clothes,' said Ellie, pulling

off her kirtle and slipping my nightgown on. 'It would be strange to see a Maid of Honour outside at this hour.'

She had soon got me undressed. Her kirtle was much too short on me, of course, for it used to be mine until I grew too tall. As soon as she had sorted out my discarded clothes and rammed her cap on my head, she dived into my bed and snuggled down. 'You don't look as good as me, of course,' she said, 'but you'll have to do.'

'If you can take my place, then I can take yours just as well,' I told her, putting the key to the workshop in a pocket. I bent my knees so that the kirtle would not look too ridiculous, and wobbled round the room, curtsying at the bottom of Mary's bed. 'Miss Ellie Buntin' at yor service, moy laydee,' I said. I know I am not the best at accents but the wretched girl need not have snorted.

Then the door opened and in floated Lady Sarah. Ellie pulled the sheet hurriedly over her head. I stuck my head in the clothes press, took out one of my shirts and made quickly for the door, holding it up to hide my face. As I went, I heard Sarah's voice: 'Grace! Are you awake, Grace? I must tell you what Daniel said about my hair tonight. Grace?'

All I heard was a very loud rumbling snore from Ellie. I must remember to tell her that I do not snore like a hog! In fact, I do not believe I snore at all!

As soon as I was safely out of the bedchamber, I realized that in my hurry I had forgotten to bring any light with me. Well, there was nothing to be done. I could not go back now. The journey was easy in the long twisting passageways of the palace, for there were rush lights everywhere. In fact I had to pull Ellie's cap well down to shield my face from courtiers who might recognize me. It was almost a relief to be out in the dark. Thank goodness for the moon (even though it will excite Mr Cheshire's love-addled brain!), for I was able to see enough to find my way to Mr Urseau's workshop.

It was dark inside and there was no sign of Masou. The high windows hardly allowed any moonlight into the room and the clocks seemed to be staring at me. I had not noticed before how silent they were. It was almost as if they had died too, with no Royal Clockmaker – or apprentice – to wind them back into life. The clock we had come to inspect stood tall and imposing on its heavy wooden cabinet, with the inlaid Tudor rose on the door. I thought again that it was a fitting present for the Queen.

I was a little sorry that I had arrived before Masou. I must note firmly here that it was not because I was scared on my own in the dark in a place where a corpse had lain not many days before, but because I wanted to get on with solving the mystery. After all, I might have the luxury of time, but Charles did not.

At last Masou appeared with a candle and I ran at him so eagerly he nearly jumped out of his skin! (It serves him right. He has often tried to frighten *me*!) When he had recovered, he held the flame out and inspected my tiring woman's clothes.

'By Shaitan, Ellie Bunting, how you have grown!' he mocked. 'You will soon be as tall as your mistress – and much more beautiful, although that will not be difficult, for she is more like a hobgoblin than a Maid of Honour.'

I would have chased him round the workshop if he had not been carrying the candle.

'This is no time for your nonsense!' I declared. 'Do you have the key?'

'How could you doubt it?' Masou grinned, delving into his pocket and producing it. 'And I wager you did not see me take it from Mr Hatton.'

He held up his hand. 'No, you can plead all you like. I will not reveal how it was done.'

'I am not interested in your methods,' I insisted. 'I just want to solve this mystery.' Actually I was bursting to know how he'd managed it, but I was not going to tell him that!

I took the little key and we went over to the clock.

'I hope I am right about this,' I muttered, and pushed the key into the hole. It slid in smoothly. I took a deep breath and turned it. There was a gentle click and the glass case opened. I looked at the instructions on the parchment.

'I must set the hand to twelve,' I told Masou. 'Though I cannot imagine why.'

I reached up and gently moved the hand round so that it pointed directly upwards. We heard some loud metallic clunks from within the clock; the first chime sounded and then, to my surprise, a wooden shelf below the face opened out and nearly bumped me in the chest. Two golden figurines popped up from the shelf, turning and swaying in time to the chimes as if they were dancing. I looked closely. One was a monarch in crown and robes; the other was a bent old man with a scythe and hourglass.

'It is Her Majesty and Old Father Time,' I realized. 'How enchanting! It is saying that the Queen is equal to time itself.'

The twelfth chime sounded and the figures clattered back down, the shelf slid back inside and the glass door covering the face clicked shut. I hoped the chimes had not alerted anyone to our presence, but then I suppose these clocks must chime quite frequently of their own accord.

'Ingenious!' Masou said. 'The Queen will love it. But I do not see how this helps us solve any mystery at all.'

'Nor I.' I was puzzled. The glass case was locked again. It had some sort of mechanism that did this. I unlocked it, set the hand again and kept my eyes on the shelf as it appeared. This time I saw something flash out beneath it, like an adder's tongue.

'Did you see that?' I asked.

'I did indeed,' said Masou, holding his candle up to the clock case. 'Some manner of spring device, I believe. Set the hand again and I will grab it.'

I stood to one side and moved the hand for a third time. Masou pounced like a cat and caught the contraption beneath. He held it firmly while we inspected it. It was a cylinder like a sconce that held a candle, but it lay on its side, and attached to the other end was a spring which had made it dart out.

'It is a strong mechanism,' said Masou. 'And it wants to crawl back inside the clock. Is it part of the workings?'

'I do not believe so.' I peered more closely. 'It looks as if it should hold something – something long and thin. But what could that be?'

'Decide quickly, Grace, for this will take me into the clock with it!' Masou's knuckles were white with the strain.

'It must be another surprise to entertain the Queen,' I said. 'Flowers perhaps. Mayhap there is something here we can put in instead.' I cast about the workshop for an object to put into the contraption and test my theory.

'I can hold on no longer!' cried Masou. 'This will do.' With his free hand, he rammed the handle of a pointed tool from a nearby shelf into the contraption and let it go. The shelf and tool disappeared inside the clock and the door clicked shut.

And then, with cold horror, I knew exactly why the Queen had been given this clock. Beside me, Masou had already taken the key to unlock the glass face and was now moving the hand round again to twelve.

'No!' I shouted. I lunged forward and grabbed him, pulling him back as the point of the tool flashed towards him. The tool flew across the room and clattered to the ground.

'Allah be praised . . .' whispered Masou. 'You saved my life, Grace!'

'And Mr Urseau saved the Queen's,' I said grimly. 'The dagger that killed Mr Urseau was inside this clock. But it was intended for Her Majesty's heart.'

'The dancing figures have a double meaning as well,' agreed Masou shakily. 'Old Father Time has come for the Queen. How gruesome!'

'And it solves the mystery of how Mr Urseau was killed inside a locked room,' I said. 'The clock was delivered and he wanted to be sure that it worked before it was taken to the Queen. He opened the case and put the hand to twelve. The dagger struck him and he died. The shelf and dagger holder slid back inside and the glass door covering the face shut again, leaving no trace of the evil deed – and the finger of suspicion pointing at his apprentice. I was wondering why the clock had such a big, heavy cabinet beneath – the cabinet weighs down the whole thing. Otherwise, the clock might have toppled and the blade would not have found its target.'

Masou gazed down at the bloodstain on the floor. It looked black in the candlelight. 'I would have been lying there too,' he murmured, 'if you had not been so quick, my clever lady, and pulled me away.'

'There is indeed a treasonous plot afoot,' I said. 'And Mr Urseau tried to warn us of it. For now I am sure that his final words *were* "the Queen". And that poor Charles Doute is innocent.'

The Twenty-ninth Day of September, in the Year of Our Lord 1570, Michaelmas

Just before the noontide meal

My bedchamber is full of Lady Sarah and yet another sonnet, so I have come to the Queen's Closet above the Chapel. It is very quiet, and I think I shan't be disturbed. It may be called the Queen's Closet but Our Majesty uses the King's Closet beside it when she comes to pray, for she is the Sovereign.

What a morning it has been! I was up with the sun but this is the first opportunity I have had to make a record in my daybooke. We will be called at any moment to go to the noontide meal but I must write everything down, for I do not want to forget a single word.

After I'd told Ellie everything I had learned and broken my fast, I went directly to Her Majesty to show her the parchment that had been sent with the clock. She was in the Paradise Chamber, and for once had no State matters to attend to. I was not surprised that she had chosen to spend a few hours here: it is a lovely room and she is very proud of its newly gilded ceiling. However, I was amazed to see it so empty. Not a minister in sight. Mrs Champernowne and Lady Anne Courtenay sat sewing by a window and that was it, apart from the Guards at the door. The Queen was seated by another window, using the sunlight to read by. She looked up from her book as I was shown in, and a frown creased her forehead when I asked for a word in private.

'I hope you have good reason for disturbing me,' she said, putting aside her volume of poems.

Speaking in a low voice so that the good ladies would not hear, I told her what I had discovered about the clock and its hidden, murderous intent.

'So although it seemed impossible, Mr Urseau was indeed stabbed when he was on his own in a chamber locked from within,' I finished. 'May I dare to beg Your Majesty to consider the plight of Charles Doute? From what I have discovered, he would seem to be innocent.'

The Queen looked at me for a long moment. 'I am most displeased with you,' she said at last. I waited to be berated and then dismissed. 'I can see by your expression that you fear my reply, god-daughter,' Her Majesty went on sternly. 'And well you might. You have been putting yourself in danger in your quest for the truth.'

I almost smiled with relief at this. I did not mind being chided – the important thing was that the Queen believed me!

My Liege continued, 'Some clever and devious mind devised this clock with its deadly intent. Suppose they became aware that you suspected them? Mr Urseau would not be the only one lying in a church crypt and— That thought is not to be borne.'

I felt very guilty that I had risked much more than the Queen could imagine – scurrying about at night to meet conspirators, and going to face a possible assassin with just Ellie and a plank of wood for protection!

Then Her Majesty took my hand. 'But as ever, my loyal Lady Pursuivant, you saw beyond what others see, and through your persistence an innocent man will not suffer. As long as what you say can be verified, Charles Doute will be released and may take his place back in the clockmaker's workshop.'

She sighed deeply and I wondered if she was feeling sad that people wanted her dead. But she was soon her normal brisk self again. 'So tell me, Grace, who is the murderer? Who would have me dead? Who is the weak link in my loyal chain? For I am sure you have it all worked out.'

'I am not certain,' I had to confess. 'The clock was delivered by a messenger wearing the livery of Lord Sheringham. That is not enough to prove that he is the murderer, of course – but it may lead us to him.'

The Queen was thoughtful for a time. 'I would not have thought Lord Sheringham a likely plotter.' She paused and gave a humourless laugh. 'But we have been surprised before by men whom we thought loyal to the Crown. At least we can investigate this murderous clock further. I am having trouble picturing its spring device. I would see it without delay – and I believe it will be of interest to my chief minister and to the Captain of my Guard. Then we shall deal with Lord Sheringham.'

She beckoned to a page and bid him send for Secretary Cecil and Mr Hatton at once.

'Now, Grace' – she turned to me – 'pick up my book and make busy.'

This was sound advice, for we did not want the gentlemen to suspect I had anything to do with the discoveries of the day. I tried to look as if I were merely her chosen companion for the morning and it was a great honour to be given the Queen's own book to read. I am sure that the poems were very fine – much better than Daniel Cheshire's at any rate – but I was too on edge to read them properly as we awaited Secretary Cecil and Mr Hatton.

They must have been waiting in one of the pages' rooms, for they were soon kneeling in front of the Queen. I wondered who else was lurking next door, hoping for a word with Her Majesty. Anyhow, I stuck my nose in the book, kept as still as a statue and listened hard.

'Gentlemen,' she said, holding out the parchment, 'this paper has come into my hands and I believe it holds the answer to a puzzle that has been troubling me of late.'

'What can that be, My Liege?' asked Secretary Cecil. He took the parchment and studied it

'In truth, my loyal secretary, it is how a man can be murdered in a locked room, with only the one door and the key inside!'

'And you say that you have an answer, Your

151

Majesty?' asked Mr Hatton doubtfully. 'We have Charles Doute to thank for that villainy, surely.'

'It would seem not,' said the Queen. 'Come, we will go to the workshop and I will show you.' She made for the door and then stopped. 'Lady Grace, you do not fool me. I have not seen you turn a page for a full ten minutes. Well, if poetry is not taxing your brain, then come with us and see if you can solve this puzzle.'

She swept out, muttering to Mr Hatton something about 'empty-headed Maids', to which I noted him nod solemn agreement. If he only knew of my success in solving Court mysteries, all while lacking his means and men! I followed eagerly with the gentlemen and several Guards. How clever of the Queen. Now I could be involved without anyone suspecting I knew a good deal about the business.

Mr Hatton unlocked the workshop door with poor Charles's key, and we all entered. I was glad I had remembered to make sure it was locked when we last left, otherwise the Captain of the Guard might have suspected something! The Queen stood in the middle of the room and held out the parchment.

'I will read the instructions and my Maid will

carry them out,' she said. She looked about the chamber. 'That must be the clock. It is a beautiful thing, is it not, gentlemen?' She pointed to the new timepiece in the corner. I was pleased with myself that I had had the foresight to describe it to her — though I'm sure Her Majesty would have figured it out for herself just as quickly, of course! 'Move the hand on the clock to twelve, Grace, for it says here "It will reveal a delight for the heart of Our Beloved Sovereign".'

I stepped up and tried to open the glass case and then realized that I had not been so clever after all. The clock had locked itself again, of course. I had the key in the purse at my waist, but Mr Hatton believed he had it in his safekeeping. What was I going to do? My involvement must not be suspected.

At once he began to fumble with the pouch on his belt. 'I believe I have the key that opens the clock,' he announced. 'There was one in Mr Urseau's hand when he died. It was small like the lock here, and if I am not mistaken, it should fit.'

It was lucky that I was facing the clock so Mr Hatton did not see me slip my hand into my purse. I had the key in my fingers — but how to get it into his? The Captain of the Guard had now emptied his pouch and was pushing around the various objects looking for the key.

'I do not understand,' he said. 'I have carried the key since the murder, but I cannot find it.'

He turned to the Queen and I took my chance. No one was looking at me so I threw the key to the floor at his feet. It made a clatter.

'What is this?' I gushed, bending quickly to pick it up. 'I saw it fall from the folds of your sleeve, sir. Could this be the key you seek?'

I tried to keep a sweet and innocent expression on my face. Mr Hatton, not suspecting a thing, took the key and put it in the lock. The glass case swung open.

'Thank you, Lady Grace,' he said, looking rather embarrassed. There was a flicker of a smile on the Queen's face. She must have guessed that I had the key — otherwise, how would I have found the secret of the clock?

I moved the hand to twelve and soon heard the familiar clunking. Out came the shelf with its dancers, and, underneath, the evil spring-mechanism. I remembered to let out a cry of surprise, which was not hard as the sprung device leaped at me before disappearing back inside.

'By the Devil!' exclaimed Mr Hatton, his

hand going straight to the hilt of his sword.

'Indeed,' said the Queen. 'I believe that on the last occasion the clock was opened, that device held a dagger. You saw the strength of the thrust. The dagger plunged into Mr Urseau's chest and stayed there.'

'And it was intended that you, Our Gracious Majesty, should be the one to receive it,' said Mr Cecil in horrified tones. He shook his head. 'What evil deeds some men do seek to practise. God was on England's side that day. I give thanks for the safekeeping of my beloved Queen.'

'Thank you, my faithful Secretary,' said the Queen. She turned to Mr Hatton. 'So this is how Mr Urseau came to be murdered, while alone inside a locked room. Charles Doute is as innocent as he claims.'

'He will be released immediately.' Mr Hatton was grim-faced. 'But who is behind this outrage?'

'The clock is a gift from Lord Sheringham,' said the Queen, pretending to read the parchment again. 'I would not have thought it of him. He is not an obvious plotter. Nevertheless, I would have him brought here and confronted with his deadly device.'

Mr Hatton issued orders to one of the Guards.

Then he went back to the clock. He tried to open the case again and seemed pleased that he could not. 'As I hoped. It has a locking device. This key is needed to open it.' He put the key back in his pouch. 'Now no one else can be hurt by it.'

We waited in tense silence for the arrival of Lord Sheringham. The Queen had an icy look on her face that froze my heart. It is unbearable to contemplate the existence of people who wish her such ill.

The Guard at the door announced Lord Sheringham and he strode in, a huge smile on his face when he saw that the Queen was present. I have seen my lord about the Court. He is an elderly gentleman, red–cheeked and good–humoured – so I had *thought*. After bowing deeply, he rushed over to the clock.

'It has arrived,' he said, patting the wood. 'I had not realized it had already been delivered. Your Majesty, I hope your presence here in this humble workroom means that you are pleased with my gift.'

'Pleased?' thundered the Queen. 'I cannot believe you, sirrah!'

Lord Sheringham fell to his knees in the face of

her displeasure; he looked dumbfounded.

But the Queen was not yet finished with him. 'You bring this killing machine into my presence and expect me to be pleased?'

'Killing machine?' Sheringham spluttered. 'I do not understand . . .' He looked up at Her Majesty, his confusion and terror seeming real enough to my eyes. 'I feared the clock might not be splendid enough for you, but . . . killing machine? I know not of what you speak, Gracious Liege.'

'I am referring to the dagger that sprang out of your gift,' hissed the Queen. She was furious. 'The dagger that was meant for me, but by sheer chance killed my loyal clockmaker instead.'

'No, no,' wailed Lord Sheringham, his plump cheeks wobbling in distress. I knew exactly what caused it – those guilty of treason faced the most severe punishment while confined in the Tower. It would only stop when Mr Hatton was satisfied that the prisoner had divulged every single detail about the plot in question. It was a dreadful thing to contemplate.

'It cannot be,' Sheringham was saying. 'It was to be a gift to show my esteem.'

'Esteem?' roared the Queen. 'It is a funny way to show it, by murdering your monarch!'

Hatton and the other Gentlemen and I were all standing as still as statues, our eyes going from the Queen to Lord Sheringham.

She looked hard at the trembling man. 'You have always been a true servant to me until this moment,' she said, her voice quieter but as stern as before. 'Tell me about the commission of this clock.'

'I wanted to give you a magnificent gift,' said Lord Sheringham. 'But I could not decide what to choose. For you are our sun and the centre of our very universe. I told a young friend of mine about my dilemma. He was most helpful, and suggested a clock. I thought this was a wonderful idea, and told him I would speak to Mr Urseau at once. But Sir Thomas said that, if I wished to keep the gift a secret, it would have to be made *away* from the Court.'

'Sir Thomas?' demanded Mr Hatton. He loomed over the old man.

'Sir Thomas Cartwright, sir,' quavered Lord Sheringham. 'He told me that the finest timepieces come from Nuremberg. I had no idea how to go about arranging this. I mean, it is so far away . . . But again, Sir Thomas was *insistent* that he could organize all this for me.'

'That was kind of him,' said the Queen. Her eyes were cold with fury and I was thankful that her gaze was not on me.

'Clocks are his passion, Your Majesty,' explained Lord Sheringham. 'He knows all about the inner workings and told me about it at great length. I confess it did not interest me, but I was grateful that he could ensure that the clock I gave you would be the very best. He told me not to worry about it and to leave all the details to him.' Lord Sheringham gulped hard. 'I never thought it would . . .' He tailed off.

'No,' said the Queen quietly, 'I believe you did not. However, it would seem that your ambitious young friend had other ideas.'

'Sir Thomas is certainly an expert on clocks and watches, Your Majesty,' I said, remembering one of his many attempts to impress Lady Jane with his knowledge. 'He has spoken to me about them.'

'And he has long been suspected of being involved with the northern earls and their devious Catholic plotting,' Mr Hatton put in, nodding at me.

'It is a nasty business,' said the Queen. 'You do appear innocent, Lord Sheringham – but I shall have you confined to your chamber until this

matter is resolved. You are to speak to no one during this time. We will put out a rumour that you are unwell and must be left alone. For I would wish that Sir Thomas thinks himself safe. If he hears anything of this, then he will leave Court at once like the coward that he is.' She motioned to the Guards at the door and Lord Sheringham was led away.

'Let me question Sir Thomas Cartwright,' said Mr Hatton grimly.

'And where would that get us, pray?' asked the Queen. She walked up and down the chamber. 'He is unlikely to admit he planned my murder. He will just blame Lord Sheringham, for the clock was *his* gift. We must think further on this, gentlemen. I fear Charles Doute must still linger in his cell for a while longer, considered the murderer by all outside of this room.'

I was sorry to hear this, although I knew it had to be so. I wished I could tell poor Charles that his torment would soon be at an end. I prayed that he remained strong.

I stared at the clock. It looked so innocent standing there. I went over again in my mind the moment the device had sprung at me. It was bad enough facing it when I knew it to be dormant.

And that is when I had my idea. What would it be like moving the hand of the clock, when you knew its secret intent – that inside was a blade about to strike you?

I could not say anything in front of Secretary Cecil and Mr Hatton, for my role as Her Majesty's Lady Pursuivant must remain secret. So I had to wait. It was very hard to hold my tongue. At last we returned to the Paradise Chamber. Mr Hatton and Secretary Cecil drew away a little to confer and I was able to speak with the Queen.

'I have a plan, Your Majesty,' I whispered. The Queen nodded for me to continue. 'Everyone believes that Charles Doute killed Mr Urseau, and that the matter is closed. Sir Thomas can have no notion that the clock has already been delivered and is in fact responsible for Mr Urseau's death. Otherwise, he surely would have fled the Court by now, knowing his plan had gone so horribly awry.'

'And how will that help us, Grace?' asked the Queen, looking intrigued.

'I suggest you take delivery of the clock in front of the entire Court,' I said. 'You could ask Sir Thomas to help you, since his interest in timepieces is well-known to us. And then you give him the honour of standing in front of the clock and setting the hand to twelve as the parchment instructs.'

'That is spectacular, my wonderful god-daughter!' exclaimed Her Majesty. Secretary Cecil and Mr Hatton turned at her words and looked at me with a puzzled air. The Queen patted my cheek. 'Tell me more of this sonnet,' she said quickly.

They turned back to their conferring, Mr Hatton shaking his head at a foolish Maid bothering the Queen with such trivial things at a time when traitors were at Court, plotting her demise.

'You have the answer to our dilemma,' murmured Her Majesty. 'I will make a show of receiving the clock as the gift it was intended to be. Sir Thomas is the obvious choice to set the hand, as only an expert like him can be trusted with the mechanism. Of course, he will do it willingly if he knows nothing of the dagger within.'

'Or he will find every excuse under the sun to avoid the blade that he is sure will be flying towards his chest,' I added. 'And his guilt will be evident for all to see.'

The Queen gave orders for the Court to

assemble for an audience in the Great Hall after dinner, whereupon I took my leave and came to write this entry. I do not know how I will sit through the meal, although I am very hungry as usual. I will avoid Sir Thomas like the plague. He must have no idea of what is to come.

Before supper, about five of the clock

Faugh! I still have not managed to find the source of this terrible smell in my chamber. It persists like Her Majesty's dog Ivan after catching a whiff of a hare in the grounds! I hope it doesn't cause me to faint from the fumes before I have time to write my account of this afternoon. And what an afternoon it has been – I can scarcely believe what happened in the Great Hall!

After dinner the whole Court was summoned to Her Majesty. She made sure I was positioned beside her Chair of State. I couldn't stand still for fear and excitement. I scarcely dared hope that I was close to solving this most puzzling of mysteries. I searched the crowd for Sir Thomas Cartwright. He had positioned himself next to Lady Jane (he truly is tenacious!). Could I detect a gleam of excitement in his eyes? I wondered. I looked away. I knew he must not catch me staring.

The clock had been placed before the Queen, polished to a dazzling shine and ready for the planned ceremony. Now that I was able to see it out of the dingy light of the workshop, I realized how magnificent it really was – yet the thought of its true purpose made me shudder.

The Queen had changed her gown for the occasion. She wore her black one with gold braids, fleurs-de-lys, and black and gold jewellery. She looked more splendid than ever as she rose to address us.

'A gloom has been cast upon my Court of late,' she began. 'Nicholas Urseau was struck down by the hand of his own apprentice and we have mourned the passing of that good and faithful servant. But today we will see something to lighten all our spirits. I wish my Court to share in the wonder of this finely crafted clock given by my Lord Sheringham.'

There were mutters of admiration, and several heads turned to look for the old man.

'Alas,' the Queen said over the voices, 'I am most

sad that Lord Sheringham is ill and unable to present his gift himself. But he sent word that he would not delay my joy. I am certain that Mr Urseau would have found much to marvel at in the workmanship we see before us.'

How clever of Her Majesty, I thought to myself. She was implying that Mr Urseau never actually *saw* this clock, although she was not actually saying that outright. So Sir Thomas would surely have no doubt that the gift had just arrived – and that his evil surprise still awaited its cue. I sneaked another look at him. He merely wore an expression of interest. Well, my devious sir, I thought, we will see how long you remain calm.

'This is no ordinary clock,' the Queen went on, and she beamed just as if she really had been given a precious gift and not an instrument of death. I am not sure that I could have kept my countenance half so well!

'A most mysterious note accompanied it.' Her Majesty held up the parchment and read the innocent-sounding instructions aloud. When she had finished, she smiled benevolently upon us all. 'Clever Lord Sheringham,' she said. 'He knows how much I love a puzzle.' I could see some courtiers who were deep in the crowd pressing forward.

No one wanted to miss this moment.

'Now, whom shall I honour with the task of setting the hand to twelve for me?' The Queen looked around as if she could not decide who to choose. 'Whom shall I trust to reveal the delight for my heart?' She put a finger to her chin as if considering the matter deeply. I thought my heart was about to burst straight through my stomacher. The suspense was dreadful! I cast a brief glance at Sir Thomas but I could not read his expression. I guessed he must be feeling horrified that the Queen was not going to be the clock's victim, and there was nothing in the world he could do about it. If he was truly guilty, that is. We would soon see.

And I did not have long to wait. His calm features soon turned to panic when the Queen's eyes finally lighted on him.

'Sir Thomas!' she said cheerfully. 'Who better to be my gallant knight? Your love of clocks makes you the perfect choice. Step up beside me without delay, my good man!'

Sir Thomas had turned quite white by now. I wondered if he was going be able to put one foot in front of the other without falling. But he seemed to rally, making a deep bow and walking slowly to join Her Majesty in front of the clock.

'What is the matter with the man?' Lady Sarah hissed in my ear. 'You would think he was going to his own execution!'

Little did Sarah know how near her words were to the truth!

'I expect he is nervous before His Liege,' said Lucy Throckmorton, nodding wisely.

Sir Thomas cunningly positioned himself so that he was to the Queen's right, and slightly to the side of the clock. But Her Majesty was having none of that.

'If you are to be my deputy, I would have you do it aright, so that you may fully share my surprise!' she said, playfully taking his arm and steering him to her other side. Now he was directly in front of the clock, right in the line of fire. Beads of sweat broke out on his forehead and his lips quivered. The Queen looked at him as if concerned.

'I see you are overcome by the honour I would do you,' she boomed. 'Be not of faint heart, Sir Thomas!'

'What did I tell you?' Lucy whispered smugly in my ear. 'It is simply nerves.'

'I am not worthy, My Liege,' mumbled the villain, trying to back away from the death he was certain was coming. 'Surely you yourself would wish to—'

Her Majesty waved away his protest. She had a happy smile upon her face, with not a trace of the anger that I knew must be raging inside. She signalled to a page, who stepped forward with the little key on a cushion. She took it and handed it with all ceremony to Sir Thomas. There was a murmur of anticipation round the Presence Chamber. The Queen was playing the scene for all she was worth and everyone was itching with curiosity to see what the clock would do.

As for me, I was itching with curiosity to see what Sir Thomas would do!

But, to my surprise, the wretch suddenly looked more composed. He pushed the key firmly into the lock and made as if to turn it. 'Your Majesty,' he said at last, pulling it out, 'this cannot be the key. It does not fit.'

'You jest, Sir Thomas,' the Queen said brightly. She took it from him and turned it deftly. Sir Thomas's face fell again. His pathetic ruse had not worked. The Queen flung the clock door open. 'Set the hand to twelve,' she ordered. 'And quickly – I am all agog to see my surprise!' The tone of her voice would brook no refusal.

I could hardly breathe as Sir Thomas turned the
hand of the clock slowly, so slowly, until it was
pointing directly upwards at last. The blood rushed
in my ears. Supposing he braved it out – how
would we ever prove his guilt then?

But at the moment the hand reached its goal
and I heard the familiar clunks, the miserable man
could stand it no more. He fell to his knees to
duck the deadly dagger that he was sure was
coming. The shelf shot out as the chimes began
and the two little golden figures bobbed and
swayed before Her Majesty. Sir Thomas looked up
wildly, sweat pouring down his face. There was no
dagger to be seen. But someone had set a feather
into the device. It shot out and dangled over Sir
Thomas's head. I was so relieved at the tension
breaking that I almost laughed. I warrant Her
Majesty had something to do with that!

No one was interested in the clock now. All eyes
were on Sir Thomas, who whimpered in a heap at
the Queen's feet. Her Majesty looked down at
him, her eyes burning with the coldest fury I had
ever seen.

Sir Thomas knew he had been the victim of a
brilliant deception. My plan had worked. But
would he deny any involvement? I sagged with

relief as he began to bluster.

'Your Majesty,' he burbled, 'the dagger . . . it was not my idea . . . I had no choice . . . I was made to do it . . . tricked by those I considered friends . . .'

There were gasps of astonishment around the Court.

'Silence!' roared the Queen. 'I will hear no more from you. Traitor! An innocent man's blood is on your hands. There was a dagger, as you say, intended to strike *me* in the heart. But my clockmaker took his duties very seriously, God rest his soul, and he was your victim instead.' She smiled grimly. 'Be sure of this, Thomas Cartwright – you will meet the same fate as all who plot to kill their monarch.'

Two Gentlemen of the Guard stepped forward smartly and hauled the villain to his feet. 'I am no willing traitor, Your Majesty,' he whimpered. 'I am your loyal servant.'

'You will be taken to the Tower, where you will meet some gentlemen who are *truly* loyal to their monarch,' said the Queen in a low, menacing voice that chilled the air. 'They do not like traitors. I am certain that they will enjoy helping you to remember the names of every single one of your fellow conspirators.' She turned away in disgust. 'Get this man from my sight immediately!'

We could hear the prisoner's desperate protests as he was dragged away. I am sure he was wishing now that he had received a dagger in the heart instead of the torture and death that awaited him.

A hubbub of mutterings flew around the Presence Chamber. The Queen gave me a special smile which filled me with happiness. I knew just what it meant. We were secret conspirators ourselves, only our — decidedly more honourable — plot had been more successful than I could have hoped. She was thanking me for my part in it. I smiled back.

Then Her Majesty quickly silenced the chatter and ordered Mr Hatton to have Lord Sheringham released without delay.

'And I would have poor Charles Doute freed from his place of imprisonment,' she announced, 'for he is innocent of his master's death. The true culprit has been found.'

I wanted to cheer the roof off the palace, but I had to stay calm, for why would a Maid of Honour be interested in the wellbeing of the clockmaker's apprentice?

A few moments after Mr Hatton had withdrawn, bowing, there was a terrible commotion outside. We could hear men shouting, and hurried orders being given. A messenger ran in and spoke breathlessly to the Queen. I was close enough to overhear.

'Sir Thomas is dead,' the man said softly.

The Queen's eyes flashed. 'How?' she demanded.

'A crossbow bolt lodged in his heart,' the messenger said, 'as we were taking him away from the palace grounds.'

'I have no doubt,' the Queen commented, 'that it was his fellow conspirators, keen to keep their names from his lips at the Tower.'

The messenger bowed. 'Mr Hatton has sent men to search for the killer.'

Then Mrs Champernowne came bustling up with Carmina, Lucy and Sarah, flapping as she herded us all back to the safety of the palace, which meant that I heard no more of what happened.

I felt a terrible fear in my heart. The evil men who planned this dreadful deed could still be nearby — and would surely plot again to kill Our Sovereign.

And just as I was thinking these dark thoughts, the Queen turned and smiled at me. (I warrant she is a mind reader!) She looked very beautiful and totally calm. And I felt much better. If the Queen was not upset by these events, then neither would be her Lady Pursuivant!

Before bed

With all the tumult of the day I had forgotten it was Michaelmas! The Queen always celebrates St Michael's day with a feast and dancing. We were not the only ones of course. Mary Shelton, who is already in her bed, has just told me that the whole of Hampton village celebrated with revels to mark the end of the harvest.

'There will be some sore heads tomorrow, I warrant,' she said. 'Fran's friend Betty works in the dairy and her family come from Hampton. She told Fran that Her Majesty is always generous at this time and makes sure there is plenty of ale to reward the harvesters for all their hard work.'

We have had our own revels. Ellie insisted on dressing me in my best gown and my new sleeves made of a thin net, with embroidered diamonds and pink silk roses at each point.

The feast was truly magnificent. Her Majesty

must have been planning this for some time, even before she packed the Maids off to dancing lessons upon our arrival here. As we took our places in the Great Hall, we were pleased to find a small package for each of us. Everyone had been given a pair of gloves. Mine were pale blue velvet and very fine. I knew that Ellie would love them when she saw them.

The Queen called for silence amidst the happy murmurings.

'In honour of Michaelmas,' she said in a merry voice, 'I give you three words: gloves, geese and ginger! You have the gloves already so let us not tarry. Bring in the geese!'

And with that servants rushed in with platters full of wonderful food. Fish cooked in hazelnut sauce, baked shrimps, a pottage of meat and herbs – and, of course, roast goose.

'It is stuffed with sage, parsley, quinces, pears and garlic,' Lucy told us. I noted that Lady Jane has ceased to be interested in discussing recipes with us mere Maids. She was deep in conversation with Sir Mark Armitage, and must have had something in her eye again, for her eyelashes fluttered like mad! It seems to me that Sir Mark is a far better choice for her than Sir Thomas. He may wax boring about horses most of the time, but at least he is not likely to try to kill the Queen!

'Delicious,' mumbled Mary Shelton, her mouth full.

Lucy stroked her new gloves, which were red velvet. 'It is an old custom to give gloves,' she said. 'They represent the open-handedness and generosity of the lord of the village – or, in our case, Her Majesty. And we eat goose on this day for good luck in the coming year.'

'Why did the Queen say ginger?' asked Carmina. She sees Lucy as the fount of all knowledge.

'There will be gingerbread later, I warrant,' said Lucy, beaming at us all. 'It is to give protection against infection.'

'A sensible tradition!' agreed Mary.

'And then, of course, there will be dancing,' Lucy finished her explanation.

'Dancing!' I gasped before I could stop myself.

With all the business of the mystery, I had quite forgotten about the secret dancers and their plan to dance for the Queen tonight. I wondered if I could suddenly be taken ill and go to my bed. When we returned from the Banqueting House – Lucy had been right about the gingerbread – the Great Hall was cleared and swept and the musicians were already playing in the gallery.

I was just looking for Mrs Champernowne so that I could plead a headache and retire to my bed when Mr Morling bowed in front of me.

'Are you ready, Lady Grace?' he asked. 'We have the Queen's permission to begin the dancing.'

He turned to the Queen and made an even deeper bow. 'We dedicate this dance to you, Your Gracious Majesty,' he said loudly. 'We are determined to show our loyalty in our efforts to please you with our steps.'

The other members of the secret dancing classes had taken to the floor, each with a partner. The ladies looked a little dismayed. They all thought their partners poor dancers. There was nothing I could do. I would have to dance. And to make matters worse, the musicians struck up a Volta. It was going to be a disaster!

But I was wrong. I did tread on Mr Morling's feet twice but that was one less than he trod on mine! However, I do not believe anyone noticed any mistakes the dancers made – well, except for when Geoffrey lifted his partner up with great gusto and tangled her up in a tapestry. For the most part we all managed to keep time, remembered our steps and did not fall over. When we had finished, Monsieur Danton came and kissed my hand.

'I am sorry that we did not seem to 'ave time for your private dancing lessons,' he said. 'But you 'ave improved. You did not dance like a lost bear tonight!' I smiled. But he had not finished. 'A goat, perhaps – but not a bear!'

The Queen clapped her hands with great enthusiasm. 'Gentlemen,' she said, 'this is secret plotting that I do approve of.'

I could hardly hide my astonishment. Mr Morling had said nothing of secrets, nor of plotting – yet the Queen seemed to know exactly what the dancers had been doing! Lack-a-day! Perhaps she even knew that I had been of their number one night!

'You have all worked very hard and deserve praise,' Her Majesty told them. 'A Sarabande now, I think, and you shall partner me, Mr Morling.'

Mr Morling's face was a mixture of delight at the honour and trepidation at the task ahead. As for me, I felt nothing but relief. Not only had I managed the Volta without disaster, but I had finally solved the perplexing mystery of the clockmaker's death.

The Thirtieth Day of September, in the Year of Our Lord 1570

Early afternoon

The Queen says we are to leave Hampton Court tomorrow.

'My pleasure at being among the autumn leaves in Surrey has been marred by the events of this week,' she told us.

I do not blame her, although I will be sorry to go.

However, there has been a better end to this mystery than anyone could have hoped. After we had breakfasted, Charles Doute was brought to the Queen in her Presence Chamber. The poor man looked hollow-eyed and thinner than ever as he knelt before Her Majesty.

'You have suffered much,' she said, gazing at him with some concern. 'Mr Hatton is deeply sorry that you were wrongly imprisoned.'

'My Liege,' stammered Charles, 'I thank you from the bottom of my heart for ordering my release.'

'You were most fortunate that someone with a keen mind discovered the truth,' said the Queen, giving me the briefest of glances. 'Now, Charles, I would have your help with a problem. Sadly I now have no clockmaker here at Hampton Court and I need someone to take his place. I can think of no one better than you to step into his shoes.'

Charles Doute flushed deeply. 'I would for all the world that my master was still here and I was still his apprentice,' he said, his voice full of emotion. 'But that cannot be. To take his place would be the greatest honour.'

'I am sure you will do justice to his memory.' The Queen smiled. 'And now arise. I have something for you.'

As Charles got to his feet, a servant approached carrying a legal-looking scroll and a small clock. This clock was about the size of a tankard. The face took up most of the front. The wooden casing looked like a tower but was very plain otherwise. The only decoration was a sun and moon engraved in the metal beneath the hand. The Queen opened the scroll.

'This is Mr Urseau's last will and testament,' she said. 'And there is a part that pertains to you. *To my esteemed apprentice Charles Doute,'* she read, '*I give my precious sun and moon clock, all its workings and contents therein.'*

The servant held out the clock and Charles took it with trembling hands. When he looked up at the Queen, his eyes were filled with tears. 'Your Majesty, I cannot tell you what this means to me,' he said. 'This clock was made by Mr Urseau himself. It was his favourite. I shall cherish it always.'

I decided that I must go and see Charles before we left Hampton Court, but I would not go without my friends Ellie and Masou, for I could not have done any of this without their help – even though Ellie had insisted that Mr Urseau's last words were 'the key'. Ellie was keen to go with me, and Masou was happy when we sneaked him away from packing up all the troupe's costumes and scenery.

I guessed that the diligent new clockmaker would already be at his work and I was right. We tapped on the workshop door and soon heard the key turning.

Charles looked flustered as he welcomed us in. 'This is truly an honour, Lady Grace,' he said. 'And a happier meeting than last time you were here!'

I smiled. 'I am glad to see you in your rightful place,' I told him.

'So am I,' said Ellie fervently. 'I never thought you were guilty – not for a minute.'

Hmm. I was not entirely sure that was true, but of course I did not say anything.

I saw that Charles had the clock his master had given him on a workbench with a bunch of keys beside it. I walked over to have a look at the timepiece with the sun and moon on the face.

'What better gift could Mr Urseau have left you?' I said. 'Even I can see that the workmanship is of the best quality.'

'Yet there is something strange about it,' muttered Charles, joining me. 'When you knocked, I was about to open it, for there was a clunking sound inside as I set it down. I know that my dear master would never have left any loose workings in any of his clocks. He was too much of a craftsman for that. So what can it be?'

I suddenly felt cold. The last strange thing to come out of a clock had been deadly! Then I pulled myself together. Mr Urseau would never have any ill intentions towards his apprentice, whom he had obviously held in high regard.

Charles picked up the clock and turned it so

that the back faced us. He handled the clock as carefully as if it had been a newborn baby. I could see he loved his work. I did not think the Queen would be disappointed with her new clockmaker.

He put one of the keys into the little hole and turned it. I felt Masou tense beside me as he opened the door. We all peered inside and found ourselves staring at – nothing but the clock's intricate workings.

'I don't see anything that could rattle,' said Ellie.

'Indeed,' said Charles. 'All the cogs are just as they should be – firmly fixed in their places. This is most strange.'

He picked up the clock again and tipped it gently from side to side. We all heard something sliding about but could see nothing. He placed it on the bench again.

'There is a very thick base to this clock,' I mused. I put one careful finger in and touched a little metal plate. It moved towards me. I pushed harder.

'Allow me,' said Charles hurriedly. 'I would not want you to . . . catch your nail.'

I am sure he wanted to say, *Break the clock*, but was too polite!

Charles drew out the plate to reveal a small

compartment. A velvet pouch had been crammed into it. Very carefully he picked it up, opened the strings and tipped out the contents. Gems spilled out onto the workbench.

'So there was treasure after all!' Ellie burst out. 'Good old Mr Urseau!'

But Charles was looking anxiously at our faces. 'Do you suppose this was meant for me? What about my master's widow? Is it not hers by rights?'

Ellie snorted and crossed her arms. 'That horrible woman don't deserve it one bit!'

I smiled at him. 'The will said *all the workings and contents therein,*' I reminded him. 'I am certain that Mr Urseau meant these expressly for you.'

And so I will close my daybooke – and just in time, for I am on the last page – and prepare to leave Hampton Court. We will soon be in another palace, and perhaps another mystery waits for me to solve. I will miss the trees, however. I wanted to have at least one more climbing session. There is one thing I will not miss – the smell of the drains.

Mercy! I thought I had finished my daybooke but I find I have solved another mystery – and this one without stirring from my chamber. Ellie was just folding my riding cloak to put into my chest when she found the jug of sour milk and spinach that we left there days ago. It has quite curdled and fully explains the awful smell!

It would seem that some mysteries can outwit even Queen Elizabeth's Lady Pursuivant!

GLOSSARY

aiglet – the metal tip of a lace, which you thread through the hole

Allah – the Muslim name for God

Almain – a stately sixteenth-century dance

basil – a leafy green herb with a strong smell and flavour

Board of Green Cloth – the main administrative body for the Court. It dealt with an inquest if anyone died within one mile of the Queen's person

daybooke – a book in which you would record your sins each day so that you could pray about them. The idea of keeping a diary or journal grew out of this. Grace is using hers as a journal

elf-shot – any small, triangular-shaped stone found in a field was said to have been made by the elves or fairies and was believed to bring good luck to the owner

flagon – a large vessel usually of metal or pottery, with a handle and spout. Used for

fleur-de-lys – a stylized way of drawing an iris – used in heraldry and fabric designs, etc.

Galliard – a sixteenth-century dance

garlic – a plant, the bulb of which contains small white claves, with a strong smell and taste. Used for seasoning and for medicinal purposes

ginger – a root, with a oungent flavour, used in cooking and for medicinal purposes

harbinger – somebody who went ahead to announce the monarch

hose – tight-fitting cloth trousers worn by men

jumbal – small, flat ring-shaped cake or cookie with a hole in the middle

kirtle – the skirt section of an Elizabethan dress

Lady-in-Waiting – one of the ladies who helped to look after the Queen and kept her company

laudanum – an opium tincture in alcohol used to aid sleep

Maid of Honour – a younger girl who helped to look after the Queen like a Lady-in-Waiting

malting floors – large, well-ventilated room where barley grain could be spread out in order to sprout before making beer

Mary Shelton – one of Queen Elizabeth's Maids of Honour (a Maid of Honour of this name really did exist, see below). Most Maids of Honour were not officially 'ladies' (like Lady Grace) but they had to be of born of gentry

Michaelmas – once a 'holy day of obligation' in the Christian calendar, occuring on the 29th September. Traditionally heralded the beginning of the autumn season

mummer/mumming – actor/acting

on progress – term used when the Queen was touring parts of her realm. It was a kind of summer holiday for her

pattens – wooden-soled footwear, such as sandal, shoe or clog

Pavane – a slow and stately dance

posset – a hot drink made from sweetened and spiced milk curdled with ale or wine

Presence Chamber – the room where Queen Elizabeth received people

pursuivant – one who pursues someone else

Queen's Closet – place of prayer constructed by Cardinal Wolsey (1514–1528), then substantially re-modelled by King Henry VIII (1535–6)

Queen's Guard – these were more commonly known as the Gentlemen Pensioners – young noblemen who guarded the Queen from physical attacks

sackbut – an early form of the trombone

Sarabande – traditional dance in triple-metre. Once banned in Spain due to its 'obscenity'

Secretary Cecil – William Cecil, an administrator for the Queen (was later made Lord Burghley)

Shaitan – the Islamic word for Satan, though it means a trickster and a liar rather than the ultimate evil

small boor – weak beer

spitboy – member of the kitchen staff whose job it was to stay closest to the fire in order to turn the roasting meat

stomacher – a heavily embroidered or jewelled piece for the centre front of a bodice

tinder box – small box containing some quick-burning tinder, a piece of flint, a piece of steel and a candle for making fire and thus light

tiring woman – a woman who helped a lady to dress

tumbler – acrobat

vellum – fine parchment made from animal skin

Volta – a sixteenth-century dance very popular with Queen Elizabeth I

Watching Chamber – elevated gallery in a church from where monks could watch over a holy shrine

woodwild – crazy, mad

'Zounds – an expression of surprise or annoyance originating from the shortening of 'God's wounds'

THE FACT BEHIND THE FICTION

In 1485 Queen Elizabeth I's grandfather, Henry Tudor, won the battle of Bosworth Field against Richard III and took the throne of England. He was known as Henry VII. He had two sons, Arthur and Henry. Arthur died while still a boy, so when Henry VII died in 1509, Elizabeth's father came to the throne and England got an eighth king called Henry – the notorious one who had six wives.

Wife number one – Catherine of Aragon – gave Henry one daughter called Mary (who was brought up as a Catholic), but no living sons. To Henry VIII this was a disaster, because nobody believed a queen could ever govern England. He needed a male heir.

Henry wanted to divorce Catherine so he could marry his pregnant mistress, Anne Boleyn. The Pope, the head of the Catholic Church, wouldn't allow him to annul his marriage, so Henry broke with the Catholic Church and set up the Protestant Church of England – or the Episcopal Church, as it's known in the USA.

Wife number two – Anne Boleyn – gave Henry another daughter, Elizabeth (who was brought up as a Protestant). When Anne then miscarried a baby boy, Henry decided he'd better get somebody new, so he accused Anne of infidelity and had her executed.

Wife number three – Jane Seymour – gave Henry a son called Edward, and died of childbed fever a couple of weeks later.

Wife number four – Anne of Cleves – had no children. It was a diplomatic marriage and Henry didn't fancy her, so she agreed to a divorce (wouldn't you?).

Wife number five – Catherine Howard – had no children either. Like Anne Boleyn, she was accused of infidelity and executed.

Wife number six – Catherine Parr – also had no children. She did manage to outlive Henry, though, but only by the skin of her teeth. Nice guy, eh?

Henry VIII died in 1547, and in accordance with the rules of primogeniture (whereby the first-born son inherits from his father), the person who succeeded him was the boy Edward. He became Edward VI. He was strongly Protestant, but died young in 1553.

Next came Catherine of Aragon's daughter, Mary, who became Mary I, known as Bloody Mary. She was strongly Catholic, married Philip II of Spain in a diplomatic match, but died childless five years later. She also burned a lot of Protestants for the good of their souls.

Finally, in 1558, Elizabeth came to the throne. She reigned until her death in 1603. She played the marriage game – that is, she kept a lot of important and influential men hanging on in hopes of marrying her – for a long time. At one time it looked as if she would marry her favourite, Robert Dudley, Earl of Leicester. She didn't though, and I think she probably never intended to get married – would you, if you'd had a dad like hers? So she never had any children.

She was an extraordinary and brilliant woman, and during her reign, England first started to become important as a world power. Sir Francis Drake sailed round the world – raiding the Spanish colonies of South America for loot as he went. And one of Elizabeth's favourite courtiers, Sir Walter Raleigh, tried to plant the first English colony in North America – at the site of Roanoke in 1585. It failed, but the idea stuck.

The Spanish King Philip II tried to conquer England in 1588. He sent a huge fleet of 150 ships, known as the Invincible Armada, to do it. It failed miserably – defeated by Drake at the head of the

English fleet – and most of the ships were wrecked trying to sail home. There were many other great Elizabethans, too – including William Shakespeare and Christopher Marlowe.

After her death, Elizabeth was succeeded by James VI of Scotland, who became James I of England and Scotland. He was almost the last eligible person available! He was the son of Mary Queen of Scots, who was Elizabeth's cousin, via Henry VIII's sister.

His son was Charles I – the King who was beheaded after losing the English Civil War.

The stories about Lady Grace Cavendish are set in the years 1569 and 1570, when Elizabeth was thirty-six and still playing the marriage game for all she was worth. The Ladies-in-Waiting and Maids of Honour at her Court weren't servants – they were companions and friends, supplied from upper-class families. Not all of them were officially 'ladies' – only those with titled husbands or fathers; in fact, many of them were unmarried younger daughters sent to Court to find themselves a nice rich lord to marry.

All the Lady Grace Mysteries are invented, but some of the characters in the stories are real people

– Queen Elizabeth herself, of course, and Mrs Champernowne and Mary Shelton as well. There never was a Lady Grace Cavendish (as far as we know!) – but there were plenty of girls like her at Elizabeth's Court. The real Mary Shelton foolishly made fun of the Queen herself on one occasion – and got slapped in the face by Elizabeth for her trouble! But most of the time, the Queen seems to have been protective and kind to her Maids of Honour. She was very strict about boyfriends, though. There was one simple rule for boyfriends in those days: you couldn't have one. No boyfriends at all. You would get married to a person your parents chose for you and that was that. Of course, the girls often had other ideas!

Later on in her reign, the Queen had a full-scale secret service run by her great spymaster, Sir Francis Walsingham. His men, who hunted down priests and assassins, were called 'pursuivants'. There are also tantalizing hints that Elizabeth may have had her own personal sources of information – she certainly was very well informed, even when her counsellors tried to keep her in the dark. And who knows whom she might have recruited to find things out for her? There may even have been a Lady Grace Cavendish, after all!

A note on gifts for Queen Elizabeth

There were many real plots to kill Queen
Elizabeth I; luckily, none of them were successful.
All gifts, no matter how small, were thoroughly
checked before the Queen was allowed near them,
just in case they were secret assassins' devices. The
Royal Clockmaker would certainly have checked
any clocks that were given to the monarch. As far
as we know, she was never given a deadly clock
like the one in Grace's daybooke, but we do know
that there was a real Nicholas Urseau (also known
as Oursian), who really was Clockmaker to the
Queen: he *did* make the magnificent astronomical
clock that can still be seen at Hampton Court
today. The real Mr Urseau served four monarchs
for fifty-eight years and died peacefully in 1590.

Elizabeth loved receiving presents. It was
traditional for the Tudors to give New-Year gifts,
and lists were kept of all those the Queen received,
with a note of who had given them – from dukes
all the way down to humble grocers. In the early

years of her reign, many of these gifts were purses of money, but there were one or two more unusual offerings. Her Yeoman of the Chamber once presented her with a marzipan tower with marzipan men and artillery inside it, and the Servant of the Pastry gave her a quince pie.

It seems that it was not necessarily the cost or splendour of the gift that was important to the Queen. When she was on progress in Essex, one of her subjects, Henry Maynard, was waiting for a visit from her. He was very worried that his house was too small for his monarch and her Court. He was assured that the Queen would not mind at all as long as his wife presented her with 'some fine waistcoat or fine ruff or like thing' and that it would be received just as if it had been a very costly gift. Even to Queen Elizabeth, it was the thought that counted.

Suitors of the Queen were also very generous with their gifts as a way into her heart. Ivan the Terrible of Russia wanted her to become his wife and sent her priceless furs. He had already got through two wives and would marry five more, go mad, kill his son and finally be poisoned! Luckily for her, Elizabeth declined his proposal – though she kept the furs.

The Queen loved receiving gifts of jewels and clothes, so anyone who wanted to give her a present would ask her Ladies-in-Waiting about colours, styles and fabrics that were in favour. Nobody wanted to get it wrong and risk the Queen's anger. Petticoats, ruffs and anything else that did not need much adjustment were popular gifts. Some – probably sensible – people chose to give cloth instead to be made up by the Queen's tailor, Walter Fyshe, and his staff.

Gifts were a good way of gaining favour with Queen Elizabeth. A courtier who went to a lot of trouble to give her a special gift was Sir Francis Carew of Bedlington Manor. Sir Francis wanted to present her with cherries, which were a symbol of purity, just like the Queen herself. However, the Queen was visiting his house long after the cherries should have been ripe. Sir Francis had a brilliant idea: he had one of his trees covered with a tent to block the sunlight so that the flowering and then the fruits were delayed. And thus, when Elizabeth visited in August, he was able to give her a bowl of fresh cherries. The Queen was said to be delighted.

Unfortunately, giving a gift to the Queen to get into her good books did not work for everyone.

When Mary, Queen of Scots, was held prisoner, she embroidered a petticoat for Elizabeth. It is reported that Queen Elizabeth was pleased with the gift and that it softened her attitude towards Mary. However, it didn't stop Mary getting her head chopped off in the end!

COMING SOON

THE LADY GRACE MYSTERIES

LOOT

Grace Cavendish

The Crown Jewels are missing! Can Queen Elizabeth's
Lady Pursuivant solve her toughest mystery yet . . . ?

GENIE US!

By Steve Cole and Linda Chapman

What would YOU wish for?

When Milly, Michael, Jason and Jess move to a town in the middle of nowhere, the last thing they expect to find is a magic book – with its own talking bookworm called Skribble! The grumpy worm promises that the Genie Handbook can make them into genies in six easy steps. Soon they are diving into a world of weirdness and wonder, trouble and trickery, trying to make each other's wishes come true.

But when the wishes start to go wrong, the magic seems scarier. What is the secret of the mysterious couple watching from the shadows? Why is Skribble so afraid of them? And if the children's greatest wish of all is finally granted, will their world change for better or for worse?

A spellbinding adventure from bestselling authors Steve Cole and Linda Chapman.

ISBN: 978 1 862 30343 0

SUPERSTAR BABES
By Narinder Dhami

*The bindi babes are
destined for stardom . . .*

The Bindi Babes love a challenge!
Amber, Jazz and Geena want
to have the new school library
named after their mum. They
have a genius plan to raise funds
for it – they're going to stage
an amazing reality experiment. The sixth-form block
is turning into a Big Brother-style house for one
week only – and they're going to be the stars.

With spoilt relatives, film stars and love-struck
boys in the mix, they know it's not going to be easy
but the Babes can handle it – can't they?

From the author of *Bend it like Beckham*.

**'A fresh voice and fun
characters that girls will love'**
Jacqueline Wilson

ISBN: 978 0 440 86729 6

THE PENDERWICKS
By Jeanne Birdsall

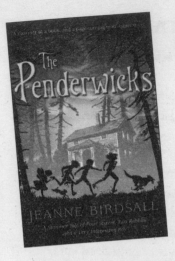

A summer tale of four sisters, two rabbits and a very interesting boy . . .

Meet the Penderwicks: Rosalind, Skye, Jane and Batty. Four sisters, all as different as chalk and cheese. When the girls, their father and Hound the dog head off on holiday, little do they know they are about to enjoy a summer that will change their lives. Instead of the cosy cottage they expect, they find themselves on a beautiful estate called Arundel. Soon the girls are discovering the magic of the sprawling gardens and treasure-filled attic, and they meet a boy called Jeffrey, who becomes a friendly accomplice in all their adventures.

But the girls also gain an enemy: Mrs Tifton, the ice-hearted owner. She gives them dire warnings to stay out of trouble – something that proves impossible for the accident-prone Penderwicks . . .

WINNER OF THE US NATIONAL BOOK AWARD 2005

'A charmer of a book and a page-turning read'
Independent

ISBN: 978 0 385 61034 6

THE LOTTIE PROJECT
By Jacqueline Wilson

*I don't want to do a boring old project.
Who wants to be like everyone else?
I'm doing a diary . . .*

Hi! I'm Charlie (DON'T call
me Charlotte - ever!). History
is boring, right? Wrong! The
Victorians weren't all deadly dull
and drippy. Lottie certainly isn't.
She's eleven - like me - but she's left school and has a job
as a nursery maid. Her life is really hard, just work work
work, but I bet she'd know what to do about my mum's
awful boyfriend and his wimpy little son. I bet she
wouldn't mess it all up like I do . . .

**'Wilson deserves her popularity –
even the most resistant page-turner would
find this difficult to put down'**
Sunday Times

ISBN: 978 0 440 86853 8

GIRLS ARE BEST

by Sandi Toksvig

Why is it his-story not her-story?
Girls have been around just as
long as boys, haven't they?

You might know of a few great
women from the past; Joan of Arc
maybe, or Boudicca or Florence
Nightingale, but . . . Did you know
there were female Gladiators called
Gladiatrices? Or that Nimkasi was the Sumerian Goddess
of Beer? Or that it was Mary Jacob Phelps who invented
the bra? Just because we don't hear about them doesn't
mean they haven't achieved amazing things, come up
with wonderful inventions or won battles!

A fascinating, witty book, jam-packed with stories and
information. Best-selling author and TV personality Sandi
Toksvig proves that girls can do anything boys can . . .
And do it better!

ISBN: 978 0 385 61524 2